It's Complicated

PORTIA A. COSBY

BROWN GIRLS PUBLISHING

Washington, DC * Houston, TX

This book is dedicated to the memory of
two very special women:
Christena Williford & Meathry Blane
I love and miss you both.

Also by Portia A. Cosby...

Too Little, Too Late

(Situations & Circumstances Book 1)

Lesson Learned: It Is What It Is

(Situations & Circumstances Book 2)

The Disgruntled Wives Club

Acknowledgments...

I really didn't want to do this because my memory is horrible and I don't want anyone to get in their feelings; but there are a few specific people I must acknowledge.

Of course, I must first thank God for my gift and for giving me the courage to share it with the world.

Victoria Christopher Murray and ReShonda Tate Billingsley, thank you for respecting my work and allowing me the opportunity to change the game with you.

Lolita, Nakia, Lisa, Rosie, Nicole, DeJuan, Carla, Leona, Orsayor, Crystal, and the lovely ladies of the 7 D.I.S.T.I.N.C.T.: Your support has never gone unnoticed. Your words have never failed to encourage. Thank you for believing in me, spreading the word to other readers, harassing me about the date of my next release, letting me bounce ideas off of you, and telling me to shut up when I thought everything I wrote was stupid.

To my supportive family members and friends...

To my die-hard readers...

To [YOU]...

You are appreciated.

So it continues for some & begins for others...

February 2007

CHAPTER 1

Vulnerable

*"The gem cannot be polished without friction, nor man
perfected without trials."*
– *Chinese Proverb*

I don't know why I'm here."

Venni sat on the edge of the leather cushion with her key ring around her finger. Surprisingly, the space was more like her grandmother's living room (minus the plastic covers on the couch) than the sterile, hospital-like setting she'd imagined. Still, the Ohio State and Stanford degrees hanging on the wall behind the desk and the absence of James Cleveland's greatest hits playing on a nearby record player reminded Venni that she was far from Gary, Indiana, far from Grandma's house.

She couldn't look the doctor in her eyes—not after completing the questionnaire that she was sure determined whether she was a lost cause or just a little screwed up; not after she'd just written down her weaknesses and handed them in like she was going to be graded on her honesty. Hell, she was still trying to process the fact that she had weaknesses to list.

And then there was the doctor. Slender and stylish. Curly hair pulled into a messy bun. Honey-brown skin that nearly matched Venni's, even though Venni wasn't biracial. Calvin Klein eyeglasses that rested just a hair below the bridge of her nose. Maybe five years older than she. A cute nerd.

It was her job to listen with a nonjudgmental ear. For most of her clients, that translated into instant trust and granted her all-access to every detail of their lives. Dr. Cox knew Venni would be different. Having already read her paperwork, she silently commended Venni for simply showing up for the appointment.

It was refreshing to have someone who didn't come in wearing a metaphoric trench coat over their words, pretending to hide something, when it was obvious they were going to snatch it off and bare their naked soul within five minutes. She would have to work hard to gain Venni's trust, and she welcomed the challenge. Charming her out of her tough exterior, down to her naked details, was going to be rewarding. It was what she went to school for. It was what she lived for.

Venni clenched her keys. She was torn. The strong and stubborn part of her refused to get up and leave. She'd committed to attending at least eight sessions, and she was no quitter. The private and vulnerable part of her was terrified and ready to flee. And that part was winning. The taupe walls surrounding them were slowly sucking the air out of the room. She knew this was a bad idea. She knew she wasn't ready.

Dr. Cox sat with her legs crossed in the chair across from Venni. She pulled a tissue from the box on her desk and handed it to her. "What do you mean by 'here'?" she asked. "My office?"

Though she was wearing her championship-winning poker face, the perspiration on Venni's brow told her truth. She swiped her forehead with the tissue.

"Your office, in this world…just…here." She held her hand up. "I'm not suicidal or anything. I'm just saying that I've been through some crazy stuff, and I can't believe I'm still here. And yeah, I never *ever* thought I'd visit a psychologist."

Dr. Cox propped her elbow on the arm of her chair and rested her chin on her fist. "So how do you feel about still being here?"

"I'm not real sure."

"Okay. So let's start with this: How did you get here?"

"To your office or to my present-day life?"

"Both."

Though her body was still present, Venni's mind had excused itself from the room. She recalled a heated conversation with her former acquaintance that took place after the girl snooped through her belongings.

"My past has nothing to do with you. Regardless of what you think you heard or read, you don't know me …"

"So you didn't witness a murder and Vance isn't your son?" Tiffany asked, taking a few steps backward. *"He looks just like you, Venni. How can you not want him with you all the time? You're so good with him, too."*

"You're playing a dangerous game. We've been tight for a few months, but this isn't a bone you want to pick. Don't let the BMW and this nice house fool you. I spent my formative years in Gary and Chicago and handled plenty bitches who thought they could talk to me any kind of way. If you were really as knowledgeable as you think you are, you would've never crossed me like this. Let me

hear you've repeated any of what you saw or heard, and you'll see the not-so-professional side of me."

"Maybe that came out wrong. I wasn't trying to offend you. It's just frustrating when you won't let me help you. You're a broken woman."

"What, and you've been sent to fix me? I'm one of the strongest women you'll ever meet. You think those little paragraphs you read tell my story? Tiffany, you are not my psychologist. I haven't asked for your help. I'm good. I don't need a textbook understanding of life. I get it. I accept it for what it is. It's unpredictable, and I've learned to live with that."

"Have you really?"

"You know what? You need to stop focusing on me, and focus on yourself. If you did, you'd realize you have issues of your own that you need to resolve before you hand out free advice…"

No one wants to hear that they need help; especially when it's insinuated it's of the psychological kind. It took three years and a nagging feeling to wear down Venni's stubbornness, but she'd always heard people say "better late than never." So there she was, seeking therapy after almost sixteen years of manipulating and being manipulated.

Tiffany wasn't the only one who'd suggested she see a psychologist. Her high school friends Keyonna and Gabriella had revealed that they'd been in therapy for a couple years and said it helped them tremendously. It was their advice that held the most weight. After all, they'd traveled the same twisted path and miraculously found a detour that some of their counterparts missed. And though they were far removed from Lakeside Preparatory School and were living "normal" lives, there were some things that still haunted them, some stops on their path that could not be erased from their minds' GPS systems. Therapy, they said, helped them deal.

Dr. Cox leaned forward in her chair. "I have to say that I'm glad you're giving this a try. I commend you for finding ways to cope on your own for all these years. You've still been able to use your potential and your skills to create a comfortable lifestyle—more than comfortable, if you don't mind me saying."

Venni placed her keys next to her on the couch. Dr. Cox smiled softly as her client slid all the way onto the couch cushion and relaxed her shoulders.

"Now, I'd like to tell you why I believe you're here, if you don't mind."

Venni shrugged slightly and held her hands out, welcoming Dr. Cox's analysis.

"I believe your self-esteem is intact. I believe you know who you are. You're not here for me to pump you up and feed you compliments. You're here because years have gone by, and you're tired of your own secrets and lies. I think you want to share your world with someone, and you don't know where to start. I think you're here because you want to be emotionally available to those you care about. As for being here in the world, the answer is simple. You're here because you're supposed to be."

Venni nodded slowly as she let the doctor's words register.

Dr. Cox continued. "*I'm* here because I want you to be emotionally available to those people and emotionally forgiving of yourself. Let yourself feel. Everything."

That's exactly what Venni was afraid of. There were perks to being numb after experiencing years and years of hurt. She clenched her teeth at the thought of fully allowing herself to feel emotions that had been denied access for so long.

Dr. Cox sensed Venni's apprehension. "It's a process. You didn't end up where you are overnight. You won't get back to where you began overnight, either. When we have physical pain, our body naturally and instinctively guards against it. We limp because our body knows that putting our full weight on a sprained ankle will cause more pain. If we want to walk normally, we have to consciously decide to defy our nature. Our mental health works similarly. After being hurt or let down repeatedly, we'd be fools to not be guarded when it comes to who we care about or who we let in. That's a natural response. But once your heart heals, you need to let it do what it does. Feel."

Venni lowered her head and used one of her hands to massage her shoulder. Dr. Cox knew that was her sign to move on.

"Before our time is up, let's lay the foundation for your following visits. I conduct my sessions using your five Ws. I call them your W-5s."

Venni looked the doctor in her eyes and waited for more.

"Who are you?"

"Venita Miles."

"*Who* are you?"

Venni sat for a few seconds. "A woman with a complicated past."

Dr. Cox scribbled on her notepad.

"What are you?"

"Torn."

More scribbling and a soft grunt. "Good one. When are you?"

Venni frowned; just like every one of her other patients did when they first heard the question, prompting Dr. Cox to do what she usually did. She placed her index finger against her temple. "Think about it. There's no right or wrong."

Still unsure of how to respond, Venni went with the year her life changed forever. "1991."

"Where are you?"

"Stuck between if and when."

"Why are you?"

After a long pause, Venni answered softly but with confidence. "Because it's time."

CHAPTER 2

Lovers & Friends

"Love is like a friendship caught on fire. In the beginning a flame, very pretty, often hot and fierce, but still only light and flickering. As love grows older, our hearts mature and our love becomes as coals, deep-burning and unquenchable."

– Bruce Lee

Since her windows were tinted, Venni decided to get dressed in her car. After a few twists, turns, and shimmies, she had changed out of her work attire, into her fitted training pants and hoodie. Just as she reached for the door handle, she remembered. She opened the glove compartment and grabbed a ponytail holder.

With her hair pulled away from her face, Venni's beauty was even more astonishing. Her hazel-green eyes sparkled beneath naturally long eyelashes, giving her a mysteriously innocent look. Mostly attributed to her 5'9" frame and high cheekbones, many people assumed she was a model or a celebrity. She was gorgeous. And even though she was far from arrogant, she knew it.

How could she not? When she went to the hair salon with her mother starting at age six, all the ladies told her she was going to break tons of hearts. Until age fourteen, her father referred to her as his angel because he said there was no greater beauty. During the weekends when she visited her cousins in Gary, Indiana, their male friends would sweat her. Hard. There weren't many girls in the 'hood with light eyes. So, they were fascinated by hers. No matter where she went through the years, she heard a compliment about one of her physical attributes, but it wasn't until she attended Lakeside Prep that she found many men were willing to put their money where their mouths were.

She was a bit vain when it came to body image and staying in shape. She loved the way she looked when she stood nude in front of her mirror, and she felt rejuvenated after a hard workout. Even though she was running late and would've preferred to go home and decompress after the therapy session, Venni jogged to the gym doors and rushed inside. She spotted Lawrence doing pull-ups nearby, and headed his way. As his chin cleared the bar, he smiled.

"It's about time," he said between grunts.

Venni smacked his butt just hard enough for him to feel a sting. "Hush."

After three more reps, Lawrence was on his feet, toweling off. He leaned in to give Venni a quick peck on the lips. "How was your day?"

"It was cool."

"Oh wait. Therapy was today. Right? How did it go?"

Venni nodded. "Better than I expected."

Lawrence smiled.

"Where are we starting?" Venni asked, clearly wanting to change the subject.

Lawrence pointed to the track above them. "Two quick miles since you didn't get 'em in this morning. Then, we'll just do core work."

As they ran side-by-side, Venni smirked a bit at the college-aged girls who nearly fell off of their respective physio balls as she and Lawrence passed. Her man was definitely easy on the eyes from his milk-chocolaty face to his rock-hard calf muscles. Every inch of his 6'3" body was chiseled and defined, though he didn't let his physical appearance define him.

He was in popular demand at the gym. Housewives, soccer moms, celebrities, former athletes, and Viagra-popping sugar daddies alike dropped hundreds of dollars for his services every week because he was the best. Five years prior when Venni joined the gym, she swiped her card to pay for a month of personal training and was a faithful client for three years. She'd chosen Lawrence because he had an impressive reputation and she was used to having the best of everything. She never expected they would become the best of friends, though.

⚮

Lawrence watched the suds slide down Venni's body as he rinsed her off. She leaned her head back, thoroughly enjoying the pampering. He loved looking at her body. In all of its toned perfection, there were clues about her imperfections scattered about. And that made her sexier—the sexiest woman he'd ever known.

The burn scars down her back, the simple-yet-loaded sentence tattooed above her pelvis, and the piercing in her most intimate place were evidence that she had a past. It took about four years for her to tell him the relevance of each, but when she did, he loved her even more.

They were only friends then. Venni's call. He wanted to make her his woman two weeks after he became her personal trainer, but she was unreceptive to his advances. At first, he thought her explanation of not wanting to date anyone was her nice way of saying he wasn't her type, but once he got to know her and spent many hours outside of the gym with her, he realized she was telling the truth. There was no way she had a man when he was always in her company.

Most people assumed they were a couple before their relationship became a romantic one. They were unapologetically close. She took him to company parties. He took her to sporting events. They went to the movies and were regulars at a few local restaurants. Two years into their friendship, they began kissing goodbye. On the lips. And they were vocal about their love for each other. But they were friends…until ten months ago on the night Lawrence raved about his date with a local news anchor and Venni felt a tinge of jealousy.

Ever the fierce and confident competitor, she had to act quickly. Before she watched her friend fall for another woman, she had to let him know that she'd fallen for him. That night, her question was simple. "How do you feel about us?"

Lawrence could look at her eyes and tell that her inquiry wasn't generic. When he told her she knew how he felt about her, she told him she wanted him to feel something about the two of them. Together. *Together*, together.

Though he was stunned, Lawrence didn't have to sleep on it. Without a second thought, the anchorwoman was kicked off of his network. And there he and Venni were, almost a year later.

Venni took the showerhead from Lawrence and returned the favor. As she rinsed the front of his body, her eyes were drawn to his lower half. He wasn't always visibly excited, but when he was, she fought the feeling to take his excitement to another level. Once she tore her focus away, she looked into his eyes.

He planted a kiss on her forehead. "You see it."

"Let's go eat," she replied before she ran her hand down his chest and over his six-pack. After giving his abs a couple quick pats, she stepped out of the shower and rushed into Lawrence's bedroom. Wrapped in her towel, she leaned against the wall with her legs tightly crossed. Forty-six seconds later, she felt much better.

Still in the shower, Lawrence turned the dial and let the cold water cool his loins. Why did he torture himself like this? He'd never met a woman who stood by her word when it came to abstaining from sex. Most chicks had a three-month rule or a give-it-up policy based on how many dates the guy had taken her on, and it was his experience that ninety percent of them defaulted after a few steamy make out sessions. Not Venni, though. The first couple months into their newfound relationship, he thought something was wrong with him, that he'd lost his appeal.

When he expressed this to Venni after an attempt to get some in the middle of the night, she assured him of her attraction to him, but reminded him that her past with men still haunted her from time to time. Not long after that, a steamy goodbye at his front door led him to beg the question again. Was she attracted to him or was he still in the friend zone? That time, Venni reached into her panties and pulled out a glistening finger. Mum was the word after she asked if he had any more questions.

So far, lotioning up sufficed, but he hoped his lady would trust him with that piece of her soon. If she planned to withhold much longer, they would have to stop the post-workout showers and overnight cuddling. His willpower was fading fast.

⬥

Lawrence's Parmesan crusted tilapia was Venni's all-time favorite. After their rigorous workouts, she always looked forward to his meals. She cooked sometimes, but she wasn't ashamed to admit he was the better chef.

Venni stared at Lawrence as he wiped off the kitchen table. She was fully aware of how lucky she was to have a man who spoiled her with homemade meals, heartfelt hugs, and a listening ear. Like an old, married couple, whether at her house or his, they ate dinner together at least three times a week and discussed their days. Usually it was more like five days a week, and the dinners turned into slumber parties.

"Can you get my sweats out of the laundry room, baby?" she asked as she placed the last few dishes in the dishwasher.

Lawrence obliged. When he reentered the kitchen, he stood toe-to-toe with Venni. She pulled the sweatpants from his shoulder and tickled him a bit.

"Stay with me tonight," he said. They practically lived at each other's houses, so his request held a deeper context.

She contemplated the proposal under the influence of Lawrence's lips. Softly and repeatedly, he kissed her neck. "I love you. I don't know how to hurt you. Let me love you," he whispered.

Though she was intoxicated by his affection, she still wasn't ready. *He* still wasn't ready, really. Venni could have sex with him, turn him out with her repertoire of tricks, and drop him like highway litter without looking back. It was a learned behavior, a defense mechanism, a bad habit; and she owned it. In her heart, she didn't believe she would do that to Lawrence. Their relationship was much deeper than the divide-and-conquer, let's-just-see-where-this-goes, no-strings-attached ones that she'd been in during her very brief stay in Louisiana. And after she left there and moved to Houston, she'd sworn off men. Lawrence would be the one to break her virginity: part two.

Venni let his hands wander a bit more as she clenched his t-shirt. Lawrence reacted with a strategically-placed kiss just below her right ear lobe, causing Venni's body to wrench.

"I love you, too," Venni replied before she slithered from his arms. She stepped into the baggy pants and pulled them over her shorts.

Lawrence exhaled through his nostrils, unable to hide his frustration.

"I do." She placed her fingers under his chin and turned his face toward hers. "Patience is a virtue."

"What if I'm running out?"

"Re-up if I'm worth it. Move on if I'm not. Goodnight," Venni replied.

After a wink and another brief tickle to his ribs, Venni was out the door. Lawrence bit his lower lip and took a deep breath. Dropped to the floor. Assumed the push-up position.

CHAPTER 3

Between Friends

*"There is a thin line that separates laughter and pain,
comedy and tragedy, humor and hurt."*

— Erma Bombeck

Fire Lounge was busy, but not overcrowded; occupied mostly by professionals who needed a place to unwind after work. The dim lighting and smooth sounds of Ne-Yo provided a cool atmosphere for dining, mingling, and some occasional two-stepping. Venni, Keyonna, and Gabriella sat in a round booth facing the bar.

"Guess what her name is," Venni said with her trademark smirk.

"Please don't say 'Coletta' or something similar," Keyonna replied.

"Nah…nothing like that."

"It can't be Dr. Salib, 'cause you wouldn't have even made the appointment," Gabriella said.

"Damn right!" Venni sipped her Long Island. "It's Dr. *Cox.*"

"That's a homophone for your ass!" Keyonna said.

Reminiscent of their days at Lakeside Prep, the trio chuckled like school girls. The years had been good to them, as they'd all maintained their girlish looks. Their ages ranged from twenty-eight to thirty, but they still could pass for new college grads. After participating in Fast Track, a specious but lucrative division of the female entrepreneurship club, their hearts and minds were reaping what they'd misleadingly sown; but the stress didn't reveal itself on their exteriors.

Keyonna raised her glass. Venni and Gabriella followed suit.

"To irony," Keyonna toasted with a chuckle. "If we don't laugh now, we'll cry forever."

"I'll drink to that," Gabriella said.

"You'll drink to anything," Venni said before she took another sip.

"Yeah, whatever," the lovely Latina shot back through twisted lips. "So is Dr. Cox old and out-of-touch?" She turned to Keyonna. "Remember Dr. Bailey?"

Keyonna rolled her eyes. "She had to be Methuselah's mother. She sat down next to me on the couch because she couldn't half-hear, hummed 'Pass Me Not' while I told her how I fell in love with dude…" She paused to think. "Oh! Girl, every five minutes, she was coughing up phlegm and spitting into a dirty hanky, told me she was gonna put me on her church's prayer list—anonymously, of course. The list goes on. I didn't last twenty minutes."

Venni doubled over with laughter. "Wait. Y'all never told me about her."

"'Cause we only went to her once! And this chick," Gabriella pointed to Keyonna, "didn't even give me a heads up. I walked into her office and was hit with the smell of BENGAY and menthol cough drops. As soon as she sat next to me, I was done. I didn't get to the humming part."

"Dr. Cox is nothing like that. She can't be much older than me. And she stayed in her chair," Venni assured.

"Did you get into the Lakeside stuff yet, or was it basic conversation?" Gabriella asked.

Venni accepted the chicken wings from their server and waited for her to walk away before replying. "I'm not sure a conversation in a psychology session is basic, but we didn't talk Fast Track yet. She said we're gonna use my five Ws as a guide for the upcoming sessions. It'll probably come up next week. Fast Track is the main reason we're all messed up. Well, I have other stuff, but you know what I mean."

Gabriella lightly swatted Venni's arm. "Look at you being all open and vulnerable. I love it."

Venni cut her eyes at her friend. Gabriella was justifiably excited, because Venni generally kept her deepest thoughts and emotions hidden. She was a human vault.

"Really, mama," Gabriella continued, "it'll feel good to let that stuff out."

"Wait. What are the five Ws?" Keyonna asked. "Like, who, what, when, where, and why?"

Venni nodded.

"Interesting."

Venni asked the girls if they had disclosed the names of the club or the people who ran it while they were in therapy. Their answer: Absolutely not. She figured as much. They all knew about physician-patient privilege and the legalities that protected their deepest, illegal secrets, but they were still cautious about revealing too much of their past to anyone. Taught in an unconventional manner, they'd learned that everything and everyone had a price. If the right person approached with the right amount of money in-hand, their secrets could be as private as an ad in Times Square.

"Lawrence knows?" Keyonna asked.

"About therapy?" Venni clarified.

Keyonna nodded.

"Yeah. He knows everything."

Gabriella nearly choked on her chicken wing.

"Everything?" Keyonna asked in a higher octave.

"Well," Venni started, "almost. We were friends first. Before we got together as a couple, I told him he needed to know some things about me because I didn't want him to only love my shell."

"Oh, shit." Keyonna downed the remainder of her tequila sunrise.

Venni leaned in and looked into her friends' eyes. "Don't trip. He's good. You know if *I* told somebody, they can be trusted."

"I need another drink," Gabriella said. "This is happy hour, and I'm losing my 'happy.'" She signaled for their waitress to come over.

Keyonna sat quietly, still in shock.

Venni addressed Keyonna. "Is it different 'cause Lawrence isn't my husband?"

Gabriella let out a hearty, "Ha!" before she ordered another round of libations.

"Antonio knows nothing," Keyonna said with a tinge of embarrassment.

Venni raised her eyebrows.

"How would he ever find out? Y'all?"

Venni shrugged. "I mean…I get it. If L wasn't my boy at first, I probably wouldn't have said a thing. I just don't want anything looming that somebody can throw in my face later. Love me and my dirt or move on to the next. Y'all know I have no problem being alone."

Keyonna sighed. "Great. So is he gonna be at your house tonight?"

"He was mounting my TV earlier." Venni glanced at her watch. "I don't know if he's stickin' around. Why? Don't tell me you're embarrassed to be around him. He's known for ten months, and you didn't know he knew until just now."

Gabriella shook her head. "He's gonna have *Promiscuous* playing through your speakers when we walk in. Watch. Aye yi yi."

Venni caught eyes with her, and they burst into laughter.

Suddenly, the sounds of finger-snaps, keyboards, bass, and Lil Jon's voice filled the lounge. By the time he let out his first "Hey!" Gabriella had strutted to the dance floor. She blended right in with the others, bouncing her shoulders and snapping her fingers. Though she started out dancing solo, she had a few fans ready to swarm.

One gentleman, a fellow Latino dressed in a military green button-down and black jeans, made it to her first. He looked to be in his early twenties, but he would've never known she was turning thirty in less than a month the way she hung with him. Gabriella was in vixen mode, whipping her long black tresses and incorporating her Shakira-hip-tricks into her rhythmic rock.

Keyonna and Venni watched from their table. Once they finished their drinks, they would be right out there with their party-starting friend. Keyonna and Gabriella were only in town for two days, on business, and this was their last night. Even though Venni had to be at work by nine the next morning and her girls' flight was departing for Orlando at seven-thirty, they were gonna make that Tuesday feel like a Friday, and regret it when their alarms went off. Happy hour was about to turn into a happy night.

They sashayed through the door at 2 a.m. Gabriella stopped at the living room and fell backward onto the couch. "I'm gonna need Tylenol in the morning. Do you have Tylenol?" she asked.

"Yeah, but you need water," Venni replied as she hung her coat in the closet.

Keyonna threw her purse onto the floor and sat on the other couch. She pulled a chenille throw from the nearby basket and draped it over her. A couple minutes later, Venni joined them with three water bottles in-hand. She distributed the drinks and sat on the floor with her back against the chair. She slid the remote off the coffee table and turned on her sound system. *The Emancipation of Mimi* album played softly in the background while the ladies wound down from their night out.

"I love that!" Keyonna said, pointing to the mink area rug in the middle of the floor. "When did you get it?"

Venni stroked the fur. "Back in September."

Keyonna leaned down and ran her fingers through it. "Gabi, feel this! I don't think I've felt anything this soft." Gabriella groaned and rolled over to view the rug. Barely opening an eye, she gave it a "thumbs up."

"For as much as I paid, you'd think it was made of angel hair."

"That's the kinda stuff ballers say," Gabriella muttered.

Venni shook her head. "Nah. That's the kinda stuff people who were bored on a Saturday with too much money in their wallet say."

Gabriella sat up to open her bottle of water. "Oh, my God! Is that Vance?" she asked. Her eyes were fixed on the 10x13 photo set on the mantle across from her.

Venni also looked at the photo and smiled proudly. "Yep. This year's basketball picture. His school pic is in the foyer."

Keyonna turned her neck and looked at the handsome boy. "He looks more and more like you the older he gets, girl."

"It's crazy. Right?" Venni replied.

In a delayed reaction, Keyonna covered her mouth. She slowly removed her hand and spoke with a whisper. "Where's Lawrence?"

Venni waved Keyonna off. "He's upstairs asleep, girl. If he isn't asleep, he didn't hear you. And there's nothing wrong with my nephew…" She held up her hands and made air quotes. "… looking like me."

"When do you get to see him again?" Gabriella asked.

"Hopefully within a couple weeks. I told him I'd be at the championship game if his team makes it."

"You're so good to him," Gabriella said.

Venni shrugged. "Can you believe he'll be sixteen in a couple weeks?"

Keyonna gasped. "Driving age?"

"Right," Venni replied.

They talked for another half hour. Keyonna shared the latest about her eleven-year-old daughter, Mya. She'd officially hit puberty with the arrival of her period. She was only two months in, and Keyonna was already over the mood swings and hygiene speeches. Jasmine was barely into her second year of life, but thought she ruled the household. Keyonna was convinced that having two daughters was her earthly punishment for the poor choices she made during her teenage years.

When Keyonna felt herself dozing, she looked at the clock. "Girl, it's going on four."

Venni laughed. "Y'all might as well shower and head to the airport."

"Pretty much. I'll go get ready and come wake her up," Keyonna said as she stood and folded the blanket. She shook her head at snoring Gabriella, who was curled in the fetal position with her hand wrapped around the half empty water bottle. "And you need to go upstairs and lay with your boo. You know he's rolled over a few times, wanting some mid-night lovin'."

Venni got up from the floor slowly and sat on the edge of the chair. "Doubt that."

"Y'all fightin'?"

"You won't believe this," Venni said, prompting a frown from Keyonna, "but we haven't had sex."

Keyonna stood, mouth agape. Venni went on to explain.

"Y'all haven't done *anything*?" Keyonna asked.

"Shower, sleep, and kiss."

"Aww...That's sweet. Intimate. Wow, V. And he hasn't tried to?"

"Please. He tries at least once a week."

"Shower...So wait. You've seen the package. Is it...?"

Venni used both hands to give the "thumbs up" sign.

Keyonna wiped her brow. "Good, 'cause it would be tragic if he was like 'Thumb.'"

Venni curled up her lip at the memory of their former client.

"No J-5?" Keyonna asked, using her right hand to simulate a hand job.

Venni laughed. Only she and her high school crew used that phrase, and she hadn't heard it in years. "Nah," she replied.

"Have you at least let him eat the pie?"

Venni shook her head.

"Oh, hell naw. You are in violation of Girl Code 00253. I can't deal with you. I'm going to take my shower," Keyonna said.

Venni laughed harder as her friend walked away mumbling. "Why tease him with that stuff if he can't have the real thing?" she asked.

"You ain't right. You've got that fine man walking around Houston with bright blue balls, and you're about to trot up those stairs and spoon with him. If you don't think snuggling your booty up against him is teasing, you need a psychiatrist, not a psychologist. Just wrong!"

Venni leaned back in the chair and closed her eyes. Sometimes she didn't understand herself, either. But Keyonna was right. She turned off the music, threw away the empty water bottles, took a Tylenol, and headed upstairs. She had about three hours to spoon with Lawrence before her alarm went off.

CHAPTER 4

Emotional Arthritis

"There are chapters in every life which are seldom read and certainly not aloud."

– Carol Shields

I'm sorry," Venni said as she entered Dr. Cox's office and sat on the couch. "I had a fire to put out before I left. Apparently my employee accepted the title of manager sans the responsibility."

"No worries. You're right on time," the doctor said, nodding toward the clock.

Venni slipped out of her jacket and set it next to her. Folded her arms. "Yeah, well in my world, right on time is late."

Dr. Cox noticed the Coach watch that peeked from under Venni's shirt cuff. "How long have you been COO at Innovation?"

"Almost a year now."

"And this is the first time you've held that type of position?"

"Yep, in this capacity."

Dr. Cox displayed a knowing smile. "You love it. Don't you? Being in charge."

Venni couldn't help but smile, too. "It's not bad."

"Mmm hmm. It's a power position. I can already tell you like to lead, to be in control. It's perfect for you."

Venni diverted her eyes. She liked that Dr. Cox seemed to be in-tune with her, but it was a little odd to be analyzed aloud.

"So what do you want to talk about?" the doctor asked.

"Aren't you supposed to tell me?"

"I forgot to go over this in our first session. Let me tell you how I operate." She pulled off her glasses. "You're paying to be here. That means that whatever is on your mind takes precedence over what's written on my notepad. The one thing we'll always do at the beginning of our chats is address what's on your mind. You may want to vent about a coworker or gush about your special someone. Some days, you might not have anything to share. The bottom line is that this is a partnership. You're not paying me to talk at you."

"I can dig that, but uh, I don't have anything specific to talk about."

"Okay. So let's start with the first w. When I asked who you are, you said, 'a woman with a complicated past.' What does that mean?"

Venni wasn't sure where to begin. Should she start with her mother dying from cancer before her thirteenth birthday or how she lost her virginity shortly thereafter? Would it be better to fast-forward to her fast times at Lakeside Prep and explain how Cole is the evil genius who made her the businesswoman she is today? In all her years, she'd never been one to pull any punches, and she wasn't going to start now. So she said what felt appropriate.

"I found out I was good at sex at age thirteen, and I turned my body into a business for about six years. I lost both of my parents before I was old enough to drive. I have a brother who acts more like a second cousin, a half-sister I just started speaking to again, and a son who thinks he's my nephew."

"What a way to sum it up."

Venni shrugged. "Call it my elevator pitch, I guess."

They began with the elephant in the room: her tryst with prostitution. Just weeks before she turned fourteen, Venni was brainwashed into thinking that spreading her legs for money was entrepreneurship. According to her mentors, receiving cash for sex made her a businesswoman. Prostitutes were streetwalkers and had pimps who smacked them around. She and the other girls involved in Fast Track worked in a hotel with bodyguards roaming the hall, and their clientele signed contracts and were serviced by appointment only.

Cole, one of the masterminds behind the operation, didn't wear flashy jewelry and call them bitches and hoes. He taught them to recognize their worth and demand their just-due. His logic made sense at the time. Every girl involved with Fast Track was already having sex. Whether it was with a boyfriend or a guy they were "talking" to, they were all having sex and getting nothing more than condom-burn or bragging rights out of it. They could all agree that their vaginas were precious, valuable. Most of their mothers had preached that from the moment each girl hit puberty. So why would they continue to give something of value away? Why weren't they capitalizing off of their natural resource?

Venni could admit that Fast Track empowered her at one time, but as she matured, she realized it had exploited her. Sure, she was able to establish a savings account that easily held more money than some adults' yearly salaries, but only after being transformed from a young girl searching for guidance to an older girl who found out she'd asked the wrong person.

"He was a smooth operator—a pretty boy. He said all the right things. Of course I recognize it as game now that I'm grown," Venni said, referring to Cole. "I still don't think he meant us any harm, though. He just meant to make money. And he did. *We* did. FT was supposed to be over after we graduated, but I know for a fact that its aftereffects have stayed with three of us."

"You're still in contact with some of the others?"

"G and Holly," Venni replied, using Gabriella and Keyonna's aliases from Fast Track.

"And does *he* have a name?"

"His name won't help you help me."

Dr. Cox raised an eyebrow and nodded. "And 'FT.' I take it I don't need to know what that stood for?"

Venni shook her head. "I've learned that details can often become distractions."

Dr. Cox respected Venni's position. She was right. The details wouldn't make or break the outcome of their therapy sessions. The doctor only asked as a way to gauge Venni's trust.

Venni's arms remained folded as her eyes danced around the room, looking for something to look at other than Dr. Cox. Her sexual history was hard to talk about with anyone outside of Fast Track. It was hard to justify how she could live that life and not recognize it as prostitution at the time. It was even harder to reveal such a humbling secret, knowing that the listener was judging you deep down inside whether they meant to or not.

"What lasting effects have come from your affiliation with FT?" Dr. Cox asked, leaning to make eye contact with Venni.

Once she succeeded, she spoke again. "Hey. You're safe in here. It's okay to look me in the eyes and say what's really on your mind. When you look into someone's eyes, you're connecting with them or attempting to. And vice versa."

Venni grudgingly tilted her head and looked at the doctor.

"If you look at me, you'll see that I care about what you're saying. You'll see that I feel something. You'll have to accept that *you* feel something about your past. And you'll feel something because you're not telling your story to a bookshelf or your twiddling thumbs or the floor. You can't hide your vulnerability from me, Ms. Miles. I know your backstory isn't some three-sentence elevator pitch that you try your best to deliver with poise. It's not that simple. You've said yourself that your past is complicated. Tell me how. What lasting effects have come from FT? And I don't want to hear about them. Make me feel them."

Venni swallowed hard and glared at Dr. Cox, who returned the gaze. Though her facial expression seemed hard and cold, Venni's words came out softly. "It robbed me of the chance to take people at face value. I don't trust anyone at first. They earn that privilege. It showed me how selfish and reckless people can be. Act first, accept the consequences later. Such a destructive way to live. It warped my views of relationships. I don't associate emotions with sex—not real ones at least. I've made many a man feel like they meant something to me for the purposes of getting them to cum and get off of me, but it was always an act. I didn't even believe in loving someone romantically until I accidentally fell for Lawrence."

She then stared at the wall behind Dr. Cox, seemingly lost in her thoughts. "I watched married men enthusiastically walk into that hotel for the sole purpose of having sex with a teenage girl who greeted them in a white shirt and plaid skirt. Sometimes, we kept our shoes on. Mary Janes." She looked back at Dr. Cox. "I can't tell you how many times I pretended I didn't know men in the dorm elevator who were with their daughters, even though they'd insisted on me calling them 'Daddy' the night before."

"Did you walk away with any positives?"

Venni wanted to say Vance was a positive, but she struggled with whether he was her blessing in the storm or a constant reminder that Hassan Salib, her high school principal, felt entitled to plant his slimy seed in her adolescent womb. Adversity surrounded his birth, from her father disowning her to Hassan demanding that he be in Vance's life to delivering him at only twenty-three weeks. It was way too much for her at fourteen years old, and she still had restless nights sixteen years later. All in all, she could associate positivity with Vance. She was positive that she loved him more than she loved anyone.

"They feel like false positives," Venni answered.

She went on to explain how she is a stickler for time because Cole drilled the importance of punctuality upon their acceptance into the entrepreneurship club. They were there to make money and to be their own bosses, and since time was money, they were expected not to waste one penny, one second.

Much of her business savvy was attributed to Fast Track and the more traditional teachings of the entrepreneurship club. She gained accounting skills, learned management strategies, and was well-versed in customer service and satisfaction.

The most obvious positive that came from the club was the money. Cole attached a high ticket to their "product," easily charging five hundred dollars for an hour of their time. As one of the client favorites, Venni made about two hundred thousand dollars in her four years—not including tips—and saved all but about twelve thousand. Those funds were separate from the mandatory college fund that Cole required all the girls to establish. Though he had no clue whether they would use the money for their education and doubted that they'd need to, it was the principle that mattered to him. He taught them that there was power in being financially stable. Mommy and Daddy's money was nice, but there was nothing like having their own.

Money management came naturally to Venni. Outside of keeping up with the latest fashion trends or taking trips to the movies on a free day, she didn't need to touch the money she made. Her father had disowned her, but she was still getting generous sums of money as an allowance from her mother's insurance policy. In addition, Hassan deposited five thousand dollars into a savings account for every month she missed working due to her pregnancy—forty thousand total. It was a number he and Cole agreed upon based on her average income, and the money was all hers once she turned sixteen.

At the end of the day, neither she nor her counterparts participated because they needed the money. Their enrollment at one of the most prestigious boarding schools in the country was proof of that. Fast Track was their thrill of sorts. They were driven by adventure and embracing of their newfound independence. However, the extra funds proved to be just what many of them needed on their way out of Fast Track.

"We still can't believe we had that much money at such a young age," Venni said with a chuckle. "But we were taught how to manage it at the same time. The crazy thing is I'm still capitalizing off of that money."

Dr. Cox squinted. "How so?"

"You learn to ask a lot of questions when three of your clients are in the banking business."

"You were wise beyond your years."

"Only in some ways, apparently."

"And you said you lost both parents before you turned sixteen?"

"I lost my mom to pancreatic cancer when I was thirteen. I lost my dad a year later to pregnancy." The lingering anger was immediately apparent on Venni's face. "He didn't die until three years ago."

"So is that how he found out about FT? When you became pregnant?" Dr. Cox asked.

"Hell no. Nobody knew about FT. I lied to my dad and said I didn't know who Vance's father was. I told Tangela that I was pregnant by an older man, but she didn't learn the whole truth about my high school 'job' until after I graduated. And that was only because she'd been around Hassan and couldn't figure out why I ever slept with him. She ended up telling Miles because she knew I wouldn't. My dad died never knowing the truth."

"And Tangela and Miles are…"

"Sorry. My sister and brother," Venni clarified.

The doctor nodded. "I'm with you now. So your father stopped talking to you because you were fourteen and pregnant. Period," Dr. Cox clarified.

"He *disowned* me because I was a 'little whore' and 'an embarrassment' and 'a disgrace to the family name,'" she said before clenching her jaw. "I became invisible to him."

Venni recalled the Thanksgiving, Christmas, and Spring Breaks she spent with Tangela, Vincent Jr., who they called "Miles," her father, and others. Her father never spoke to her, never made eye contact with her. She may as well have been a piece of furniture. By law, he couldn't put her out of the house, so she spent some of her summer vacations at the place that used to feel like home. But the majority of the time, she was at Tangela's apartment in Chicago.

"Were you close to your father before then?"

"I was a mini him. 'Close' doesn't even describe what our relationship was before Vance came along."

"Did you ever or do you resent Vance for that?"

Venni shook her head. "I used to resent his father. I still hate him with everything in me, but that's just because he's a disgusting human being. I believe everything happens for a reason. Vance's conception showed me how conditional love can be; even from those you thought would love you through anything."

They sat in silence. Venni shifted a bit in an effort to relieve the tightness in her chest.

Dr. Cox spoke up. "What are you feeling?"

"Everything. All over again. I hardly ever talk about this stuff. When I do, it hurts. I won't lie. But it goes away again. It's like emotional arthritis."

"I like that," Dr. Cox replied.

"Don't let me find out you used it in a journal article or something." Though Venni's eyes still held sadness, her smile was a genuine attempt to lighten the mood.

Dr. Cox laughed. "No way. And something tells me I don't wanna tick you off." More laughter. "But I want to build on that. 'Emotional arthritis.' It's the perfect description of what you're going through. The memories aren't going anywhere. Therefore, the pain isn't either. But you can find ways to ease the pain." She smiled. "You know what, Ms. Miles, you don't give yourself enough credit. You're an incredible young woman. Brilliant. Successful in spite of. My grandmother used to say, 'We all have to go through it to get to it.' Do you realize you're there? You've gotten to it."

"It?"

"The good part," Dr. Cox said. "You've closed yourself off for so many years that you don't have full perspective on where you are versus where you could've ended up. Once you feel safe enough to come out and smell the roses, you'll see what I mean."

Venni glanced at her watch. Though her move was subtle, Dr. Cox noticed and cut her eyes at the clock. They only had five minutes left. She closed the cover of her notepad.

"This feels like a good stopping point. Yes?"

Venni nodded and stood to put on her jacket. "I have to run to the dealership to close the deal on Vance's birthday present," she said with a bit of a smile.

"Dealership as in car dealership?"

"He turns sixteen in two weeks." She beamed with pride on her way to the door.

"What a gift!"

Venni looked over her shoulder. "Dipping into my FT money. It still spends, no matter how dirty it is." She shrugged and thanked the doctor for her time before she walked out.

CHAPTER 5

V-Day

*"Love has nothing to do with what you are expecting to get.
It's what you are expected to give—which is everything."*

– Katharine Hepburn

It was the morning of Valentine's Day, and though Venni wasn't big on the holiday, she was surprised that Lawrence hadn't acknowledged it. The only communication she'd received was a text he'd sent at 1 a.m. saying that he wouldn't be able to accompany her for their morning run because he was meeting a client at the gym. Her reply was simple: `Okay. See you this evening.`

This was their first Valentine's Day as a couple. She didn't know what to expect, but she was sure Lawrence would make it special. He made every day special, and that's why she loved him. To show her appreciation, she'd planned to cook Porterhouse steaks and lobster mac and cheese. Before she left for work, she put a bottle of wine in the refrigerator—a semi-sweet Riesling that was gifted to her by a client in France. She'd been waiting for a special occasion to pop the cork on the expensive beverage, and the day had finally come.

During her morning commute, she toyed with the idea of offering herself for dessert, but having first-time sex on Valentine's Day seemed too contrived for her taste. She yearned for the romance she'd seen in movies. She wanted rose petals and soft music. She even had a few playlists on her iPod ready when needed. She wanted to moan with sincerity, unrehearsed, and to close her eyes only because she was savoring the feeling of Lawrence's skin against hers. She wondered if crying during sex was a director's tactic to convince female moviegoers to believe in love or if women really have been brought to tears after having a soul-shaking orgasm. Could she have a soul-shaking orgasm? If so, she wanted to order five...hundred. And she wanted the ride with Lawrence to be intergalactic; to see the sun and the moon and the Big Dipper and baby Jesus. She wanted fireworks.

Regardless of whether real-life sex could be comparable to movie sex, Venni wouldn't know tonight. They were going to eat, drink, and be horny.

Venni didn't think twice about wearing her red blouse on Valentine's Day. She'd bought it Tuesday because it matched her new black pumps with red accents. She wore it because it was Wednesday and she'd been waiting to wear those shoes for three weeks. Almost everyone she passed on the way to her office complimented her. Those who knew her better than others said things like, "Look who's in the spirit today!" or "Lady in red!" or "Love looks good on you!" There was no convincing them that she didn't dress for the holiday. So, she stopped trying after speaking with the third person.

She was still laughing when she entered her office. She finished reading the first page of the report in her hand before she shut her door. When she looked up, her jaw dropped. Blue roses lined the wall to her left. White roses lined the wall behind her desk. Red roses lined the wall to her right. They were breathtaking. There was one issue, though. The decor looked more appropriate for Flag Day or Independence Day.

Three nosey employees peeped through her window to witness her reaction. Irene, the receptionist who helped Lawrence set things up, had the biggest smile of the trio. Camden, Venni's assistant, was a close second, holding his hand over his heart and swooning. Venni felt their eyes on her. She looked over her shoulder and saw eyeballs and teeth through the blinds. She pointed an admonishing finger at Camden and Irene while maintaining her smile. She knew nosey-ass Jillian didn't have anything to do with the execution of Lawrence's surprise, so she didn't even look at her. Jillian just wanted to…well, be nosey. It was her purpose in life.

Venni closed the blinds in their faces before walking to her desk. She couldn't wait to call Lawrence and thank him. There was no client he had to meet at the gym earlier. He was right in her office, showing everyone that she was the prettiest girl in the world—a title he'd given her long before they became romantically involved. He'd now shouted it from the rooftops without saying a word. Her employees had just witnessed what her day-to-day felt like.

Once she was seated, she stared lovingly at the photo of her and her boo. What a man. Before she pulled her phone from her laptop bag, she took another minute to admire the flowers that surrounded her. She dialed Lawrence and powered on her PC.

"You are so sweet," Venni said after Lawrence answered. "And sneaky. Thank you."

"You're very welcome."

"I'ma get you, though. You know the whole office is buzzing now and people are gonna be all in my business."

"You only have to deal with them for another day. They'll get over it by the time Monday comes."

Venni frowned. "It's Wednesday, babe. What are you talking about?"

"You haven't talked to Camden yet?"

"No…I have to go over this report before ten, so I came straight to my office. I just closed the blinds on him and Irene, though. I knew they had something to do with this. They were—"

"Look in your drawer."

She rolled her chair backward and pulled the center drawer out. An envelope with "V. Miles" written on it immediately caught her attention. She opened it and peeked inside. Her eyes widened when she got a glimpse of Dwyane Wade.

"Baby!" she exclaimed as she pulled two tickets for the NBA All-Star game from the envelope. One for Saturday and another for Sunday.

"Happy V-Day," Lawrence replied. "You probably thought I was crazy with the red, white, and blue flowers. Huh?"

"It makes sense now. NBA colors. I can't believe you got us tickets, baby. Wait. It's in Vegas! We're going to Vegas Saturday?"

"Friday morning," Lawrence said. "You've had Friday off since December."

"Camden's known about this since December? Oh, I've got something for his ass *and* yours."

"Shit…I hope you do. But I gotta bounce, pretty girl. Mr. Armstrong is here. I'm about to make him squat until his legs buckle."

I want you to make my legs buckle, Venni thought before saying, "I love it. I love you."

"Love you, too. Six o'clock?"

"Six o'clock."

Six o'clock came and went. Venni and Lawrence ate their steak, drank their wine, and enjoyed some cuddling on the couch. Things were hot and heavy by nine. Hands were tucked in private places. Tongues were traveling. The temperature was rising. Venni was down to her t-shirt and panties, while Lawrence was coming out of his last article of clothing. As he tucked his thumbs under the elastic of his basketball shorts, Venni stopped him.

"Baby…" Lawrence whined.

Venni only smiled and slid from under him. "Are you pouting?"

He shrugged. "I thought I would luck up since it's Valentine's Day." He reached out and tugged lightly on her panties.

From the neck down, her body couldn't hide its weakness, its desire to go further, but she was a pillar of strength from the neck up.

Venni twisted her lips. "You know me better than that. When it happens, it won't be because it's a holiday. It'll be a holiday because it happened."

Lawrence nodded as he looked into her eyes. "I sure hope you can back up all this shit-talking."

"You know I can. That's why you're waiting for it."

"I'ma be straight up with you. This is frustrating as hell, babe. To hear you tell it, you were an all-star in the game, but every time we get close to you showing and proving, you act like you're retired."

"Jordan came out of retirement," Venni replied.

Lawrence sat up straight. "Seriously, baby. What are you afraid of? Are you nervous because it's been so long?"

Venni let a chuckle slip. "Nervous? Riding you would be like riding a bike, baby. We can attribute it to muscle memory."

"So what is it? You know I love you. We've known each other for—"

"It's the unknown. I don't know what'll happen after we have sex."

"I'm not going anywhere, if that's what you're worried about. I'm not here to conquer and throw the deuces." He touched his forehead to hers. "Especially if it's half as good as you suggest."

"Please. Even the best 'p' won't stop a man from wandering off if he really wants to. But that's not my concern. That's not even in your nature."

Venni racked her brain for a way to tell Lawrence that she only knew how to "hit it and quit it" without sounding like a jerk. "You realize this is the first relationship I've been in since I was thirteen. Right? And I don't even think that counts. I haven't had meaningful sex. Roderick was my first love, but I was thirteen. We didn't make love. We fucked like rabbits."

Lawrence rubbed her thigh. "I won't fuck you like a rabbit," he said innocently.

After a few seconds of silence, they looked at each other and laughed.

Venni was grateful for their friendship. If they hadn't been friends first, she was sure Lawrence wouldn't be as patient or understanding. No man would. Who else could crack a joke and share a genuine laugh at such a frustrating time? A friend. She acknowledged that and truly wanted to show her appreciation...horizontally.

"I wanna know what it feels like to make love, and I want you to show me. Right now, my fear is stronger than my desire." She squeezed his leg. "I'm trying."

"Why don't you get down and give me thirty donkey kicks? See if that strengthens your desire."

"I'm pretty sure you watching me do them would strengthen *your* desire."

Lawrence put his hands up. "I'm a team player."

Venni crawled over to him and kissed his cheek. "We're talking about my mental state, Mr. Personal Trainer, not my physical. The desire down there is evident, wouldn't you agree?"

"I don't remember. Let me see," Lawrence joked, hiking up her t-shirt.

She playfully swatted his hands away and held them. "Thank you."

Lawrence nodded.

"That's the last time you'll hear me say it," she continued. "Actions speak louder."

CHAPTER 6

Bygones

"In a broken nest there are few whole eggs."

– Chinese Proverb

Did you find out if you can come home for Thanksgiving?" Tangela asked.

"I'm not coming," Venni replied.

"You have to! Aunt Birdie even said she was coming. I talked to her yesterday and convinced her to make the yams. And John-Boy was asking about you. He's frying the turkey."

"Nah. I'm good. They have turkeys here. And yams."

"You can't get the extra days off work or you just don't want to come?"

"I didn't request the days off. I told you a month ago that I don't wanna come. You ignored my words and said you'd give me time to think about it. I won't be there. That was my final answer then, and it's my final answer now."

Tangela sighed. "V…"

Tangela had asked Venni to join her in Merrillville, Indiana at Venni's childhood home for a traditional family dinner and visit to their father's grave. She had even reached out to their brother, Miles, to see if he would come, too. Miles had given his usual answer to any invitation: He was busy. But he at least asked Tangela if there was anything he could do long-distance to help and gave her the names of a few more people to invite to the cemetery.

This was going to be more than Thanksgiving dinner. Tangela wanted to take the day to celebrate the life of the great man the three of them called "Dad," and to announce a major surprise that was a testament to life coming full-circle. One life had ended, but another was beginning. She had been holding in the secret of her miracle pregnancy since August, in hopes of announcing the blessing to the people closest to her. She had it all planned out. When they took turns at the dinner table saying what they were thankful for, she was going to rub her belly and say, "Life."

Now it was looking like she would only announce the news to her mom, aunts, uncles, and a few cousins. Since her own brother and sister refused to come, she didn't know when she would tell them. A part of her wanted them to hear the news from someone else, but she wasn't sure who would tell them. They were loners. No one on their father's side of the family had their numbers but her. Because of age and location differences, they never had mutual friends. And she could post all the ultrasound pictures she wanted on Connect.com, but her siblings would never know. Neither of them had a profile. So much for being passive-aggressive.

When she took a moment to be honest with herself, she admitted that Miles wouldn't care one way or the other. He would congratulate her via text and continue living his movie-producer lifestyle without blinking. Once the baby was born, he would send a teddy bear and some overpriced clothing. Thereafter, it would be surprising if he remembered a birthday. But that was Miles. He was always wrapped up in himself, and Tangela couldn't say they were ever close. They were cordial…and shared DNA.

Venni was a different story. She, of all people, would understand how much this pregnancy meant to Tangela. At age eighteen during her first visit to the gynecologist, Tangela was told that she was unable to bear children due to some scarring on her fallopian tubes and ovaries. Two years later, her boyfriend of four years fathered a child with another girl while she was away at Northwestern. In the midst of her tears and break-up speech, he offered her a dose of painful rationale: "I never wanted to hurt you, but maybe it's for the best. It's not like we could've had a future together. I would've wanted kids at some point, and you can't give me any. I guess the universe has spoken."

There was a time when she loved how in-tune he was with astrology and spirituality and unseen forces acting upon their lives; but after that statement, she hated him and the universe. She was in a bad place. Bitter. Doubtful of a God who could snatch motherhood away from her, knowing she longed to nurture and raise at least three fat-faced, bright-eyed babies. She was maternal by nature—a giver—an attribute that made her and Venni's relationship what it was.

When Venni's mother passed away, Tangela stepped in to help her thirteen-year-old little sister through the growing pains of puberty. She tried her best to answer Venni's questions and give advice in a way that was sisterly, yet motherly. Most of her availability was on weekends or on days she didn't have classes, but she did her best with the limited amounts of time. At age twenty-one, when most of her friends were going to the Kappa party or to Lou Malnati's for pizza, she was driving an hour away to Merrillville to take her sister to the movies and make sure she had tampons.

Venni didn't know Tangela was infertile until she called to tell her she was seven weeks pregnant and scared out of her mind.

Tangela listened to her baby sister's fears and got her to stop hyperventilating. Venni wouldn't give her details about the father, but she kept saying, "He won't let me get rid of it." Tangela wouldn't have let that happen either way. Life was a gift, and even if Venni didn't want to keep that gift, she could re-gift it.

So there it was. Almost two years after the breakup with her longtime boyfriend, the same God Tangela had questioned because of her circumstances had given her an alternative. To her, Venni's pregnancy was a blessing. After she attended Venni's first prenatal appointment, she revealed her sterility and offered to raise the baby if Venni wanted her to. No pressure. She had another seven months to figure out what she wanted to do.

Venni didn't know how she would be able to raise a child at the age of fourteen, and she was quite sure she didn't want to figure it out. And if the child came out looking like Hassan, she surely wouldn't be able to love it like a mother should. The day she found out she was having a boy was the day she gave Tangela an answer. Vance was all hers.

Once Venni had him and saw her little survivor, she fell in love. He was a tiny thing, weighing one pound, twelve ounces. The nurses broke the rules, allowing her to sleep in the NICU next to his incubator because he wasn't expected to make it through the night. When she woke up the next morning and saw that he did, too, she told Tangela she would let her raise him with one stipulation: She wanted to be in his life, and she wanted to have some say-so when it came to making decisions for him. Tangela agreed. Done deal.

Besides her mother, Venni was the main person Tangela wanted to tell about her pregnancy. Venni had seen her tears—the ones that carried the pain of infertility and the joyous ones that fell when she first held Vance. She knew her sister would celebrate this announcement with love and joy, so she took her snub personally.

"Don't 'V' me," Venni replied. "I've never been the life of the party. You all will be just fine without me."

"What about Vance? He thought you were coming."

"Lies. I told Vance I wasn't coming last month, too."

"What excuse did you give him?" Tangela asked.

"Excuse?" Venni laughed. "I told him I wouldn't be able to make it. Period. The planets won't misalign if I don't come. Damn! Y'all have fun. Eat some of Aunt Birdie's yams for me."

Tangela sucked her teeth. "This is deeper than yams, Venni. It's about family. But whatever. Just know it's gonna look awfully shady if only one of Daddy's three children is there to dedicate the new headstone."

"You have to know that I don't care what it looks like. And he only had two children. Remember?"

"Don't start that," Tangela said, clearly exasperated.

"Tangie, I'm not doin' this shit. I'll talk to you later."

"Don't forget you still owe your part for the headstone whether you come or not. So, make sure you send the money ASAP."

"Who owes money? I didn't agree to pay for that."

"We said we would split it three ways."

"You and Miles may have said that, but I know for a fact that I didn't. You can draw his name in the dirt with a stick for all I care."

"That's real classy. You need to show some respect for the dead, Venni. Grow up and let it go."

"Vincent Miles, Sr. didn't mince words when he told me he wasn't my father anymore. You couldn't pay me to respect that."

"Right. But you used to get paid to spread your legs for strangers."

"Oh, we're doin' that? Gloves off?" Venni asked. "Just remember that spreading my legs gave you the son your rotten-ass eggs couldn't produce. I may have a messy past, but never once have I walked *around demanding respect for my dishonorable shit. That man made me call him by his first name and wouldn't even look me in the face for how many years? You can throw out all the insults you want, but my feelings about your dad won't change, dead or alive."*

"Your attitude is pathetic. Maybe you shouldn't come."

"I don't do this petty-girl dumb shit, Tangela. Fuck you and your father."

The dial tone blared in Tangela's ear. She held the phone in front of her as she tried to figure out where the conversation took its fatal turn. All she wanted was for Venni to come home for the holiday. The more she thought about it, it didn't matter. The lowest of the low blows were thrown. They'd hurt each other intentionally, and neither was ready to apologize.

Theodore thought it was best that Venni didn't come for Thanksgiving and suggested that Tangela rethink telling her about the pregnancy. Venni and Vance had a special relationship, a closeness even strangers recognized. Because of this, Tangela didn't like to go anywhere with them. If they wanted to go to Great America, she'd say she didn't ride rollercoasters anymore. If they asked her to join them at the mall, she'd say she needed to cut back on her spending. There was always at least one person who would say, "Your son is so handsome. You two look just alike," and direct the compliment to Venni.

Theodore always feared Venni would one day want Vance to know the truth of his maternity, and what better time to tell him than when she finds out that Tangela can bear her own child? He warned Tangela to be smart. Venni was in a completely different place in life. She wasn't a scared teenager who just wanted to finish school. She was a thirty-year-old top executive living in a grand house with plenty of extra rooms. She was financially stable…and she still didn't have any other children. That had always raised an eyebrow with Theodore. He felt Venni was too fixated on Vance to share her love with another child. And that made her a threat.

Theodore had expressed this to Tangela after they became serious and he learned of Vance's adoption. All along, Tangela thought his philosophy was ludicrous. He and Venni had never gotten along, and she was sure he was biased. But the bug he'd placed in her ear bothered her from time to time.

As the days, weeks, and months of no communication with Venni went by, Tangela took her husband's advice. She wouldn't tell her about their bundle of joy that was due in June. Her decision wasn't easy to stick to. So many times, she wanted to pick up the phone and tell her about a similar craving she had or text a picture of her swollen ankles or simply tell her that she missed her. Stubbornness wouldn't allow it. She kept up with her somewhat through Vance, who spoke to her at least once a week.

Tangela and Theodore had sat him down after the Thanksgiving reveal to tell him why Venni could never know about his new brother or sister. They played off of his love for Venni, saying that she was unable to have children and would be devastated to learn that Tangela was having another. Though he was a bit confused as to how she wouldn't eventually find out, he agreed to do his part. He wouldn't mention the child until his parents said it was safe.

Tangela had concerns about how things would play out if she and Venni ever spoke again. Would she keep things the way they were or say, "Surprise! You have a new niece or nephew!"? There was no way she would keep a whole person a secret. Was there?

CHAPTER 7

Effortless

*"Happy is the son whose faith in his
mother remains unchallenged."*

– Louisa May Alcott

Happy Birthday!" Venni said with a wide grin.
She waved at her MacBook screen where she saw Vance's
smiling face.

"Thanks, Aunt V," he said.

"You in the basement again?" Venni asked after she caught
what she believed was a glimpse of the air hockey table.

"Yeah. It's not as noisy down here."

"Mmm hmm," Venni said with disbelief. "Ain't nobody
there but your mama and Theodore's lame ass. What noise?
The *Jeopardy* buzzers? You want privacy. I know what sixteen-
year-old boys do. One of your little girlfriends probably just
got done flashing you on here."

Vance chuckled with embarrassment. "Nah…"

"Anyway, what did you do today?"

Vance told her that he went to Ava's house after basketball
practice and hung out.

"So you two are official?" Venni asked.

"Yeah…"

There was something devilish about the crooked smile that accompanied his response.

"What did she get you?"

He pointed to his hoodie. "And matching pants."

"A Jordan outfit? Does she have a job?"

"She works at the pretzel spot at the mall."

"And she saved probably ten checks just to get you that?"

Vance laughed. "Her mom gave her the money, I think."

Venni grunted. "That's pretty damn generous. Just remember what I told you. Don't get caught up."

Vance was a Division I prospect for basketball. It was his sophomore year, and he was being heavily recruited by universities in the DMV area as well as Kansas, Duke, and Villanova. Indiana and Kentucky had been following him since his seventh grade season, and were very clear about their interest. At 6'5", Vance was a versatile player. He had the ball-handling skills of a point guard, a jump shot like a shooting guard, and the power of a forward. He was a natural. Most importantly, he was humble.

He had been around the sport since he was two. Tangela attended most of Venni's basketball games at Lakeside Prep, and he was right next to her in the bleachers, cheering Aunt "Benni" on. Venni bought Vance his first jersey at age four— Reggie Miller, her favorite NBA player—and gifted him with his first basketball on his sixth birthday. Once he had a ball of his own, there was no getting him to put it down.

At the beginning of his freshman year when he became a starter for the varsity squad, Venni talked to him about the cons of being a sought-after athlete. She warned of fake friends, leeches, girls with sudden interest, and haters. She stressed that he needed to stay focused amidst the distractions if he truly wanted to succeed as a college and perhaps a professional athlete.

"Ava and her mom are cool, Aunt V."

"I get it. And I say wear the hell out of that sweat suit. Just remember that a lot of people are cool until they aren't. There are usually expectations attached to gifts. Ain't nothin' free."

Vance could always count on Venni for good advice. She was always straight-up, understanding, and level-headed. Whether it involved a fight with a friend or girl problems, he felt comfortable talking to her. She was more than his aunt. She was like a sister and a confidante.

She was also his go-to when it came to sports talk. He wouldn't dare mention the word "ball" to his stepfather. Theodore had only attended four of his games since he started playing—two in elementary, one in middle school, and a playoff game his freshman year. He believed sports were a waste of time and energy that could be put into being a scholar and had made it known that Vance's 3.8 GPA wasn't good enough for him. He could talk to his mom about his basketball stats, but she really didn't know what they meant. She was proud of him whether he scored six or thirty-six points. Venni knew the game and the game outside of the game, and she wanted to share all of her knowledge with him.

"Before I forget," Vance started, "thanks for my shoes."

Venni winked. "You have to wait 'til you get here this summer to get your other gift."

"Or you could bring it when you come for the championship game," he said with a grin.

Venni laughed. "Wait. I thought you won't know about the championship until tomorrow night, after your game."

"Can't a brotha think positively?"

"I'll tell you what. I'll bring a picture of it when I come if the team makes the championship."

Vance sucked his teeth. "Come on, Aunt V!"

"Speaking of basketball, guess where I'm going this weekend?"

"Not Vegas…"

Venni smiled.

"Nuh unh!"

"Lawrence surprised me for Valentine's Day. We leave in the wee hours tomorrow."

"Tell L he could've hooked me up. That's foul."

"You have your own game to play tomorrow, youngin'. I'll take lots of pictures."

They talked a bit more about his day. He expressed some disappointment about not getting a car and blamed it on Theodore. Venni didn't express her annoyance with

Tangela for letting Theodore put a damper on everything that was important to Vance, but her blood boiled from Tangela's submissiveness and inability to make independent decisions. It took every bit of her willpower to not carry her laptop into the garage and show Vance his 2005 blacked-out Chrysler 300.

"What's your mother doing?" Venni asked.

"I don't know. Want me to go get her?"

"Nah. I'll call her. I'm about to go. We'll talk before your game. Okay? Be good. Love you."

"Love you, too."

"Now get your ass upstairs and stop playing with yourself in the basement," Venni joked before disconnecting the session.

❦

The phone rang loudly on the kitchen table, startling Tangela. She put the spoon down and leaned forward to read the display. Kayla wiggled in her lap and reached for the jar of sweet potatoes that was just out of her reach.

"Honey!" Tangela yelled.

Theodore came into sight within seconds. Though he still had his sweater vest on, his tie was off and his top two buttons were unfastened. In his book, he was comfortable.

Tangela stood and handed the eight-month-old to her husband before he could say a word. "It's Venni."

He kissed the side of Kayla's head. "Go ahead."

Venni and Tangela had just started talking again a month prior. After a year and three months of no direct communication, Tangela broke down and wished her little sister a happy new year. This would only be their third conversation since then, but she was happy they were repairing their relationship. During those chats, they'd caught each other up on new happenings and major life events. Venni happily reported that she and Lawrence were a couple. Tangela bragged about Theodore's promotion that allowed her quit her job and stay home, and she confirmed that Venni knew all about Vance's latest accomplishments. No mention of a baby.

Tangela swiped the ringing phone and hurried away from her fussy baby. Once she was down the hall, she answered the call. "Hey, V."

"Took you long enough. Were you busy?" Venni asked.

Kayla screamed loudly right when Tangela entered the study. Tangela quickly closed the door. "Not really. I was just watching TV with Theodore. We couldn't find the phone."

"What was that?"

"What?"

"That noise. It sounded like a baby or a cat."

"Oh! That was the TV. Did you already talk to Vance?" Tangela asked.

"We just got off of Skype. He said it was noisy upstairs. I guess he wasn't lying. Is Theodore living on the wild side and watching *Animal Planet* tonight?"

Tangela couldn't help but laugh. Her husband was undeniably square. Unlike the guys she'd dated before him, he sat with perfect posture, wore the correct pants size, knew the difference between a dinner fork and a salad fork, and could tie a bowtie.

"I missed you, girl," she said.

"I bet ol' Theo didn't! Where are you? In the study again?"

"Yep! The bat cave," Tangela answered.

"So do you go in there only when you're talking to me or do you do this with all your phone convos? Is that one of his dumb-ass rules?"

"He doesn't have rules. He has requests," Tangela corrected. "And I come in here for most of my phone calls. Ever since we remodeled this room, I find any reason to use it."

"Well, if Vance's team wins Friday, I'll be in town for the next game. I need to see this room. It must be like a spa."

"Um…where are you staying when you come?"

"Not with you. Don't worry."

"I didn't mean it like that," Tangela lied. "I was just—"

"Stop before you trip over your words, Tangie. Lawrence and I already planned on getting a room."

"It's so weird that you two are a couple now. I'm so used to him being your buddy. I'm happy for you. You sound happy whenever you talk about him."

"I am."

Tangela was genuinely happy for Venni, but she was a bit envious that her little sister managed to win in spite of her dishonorable past. For starters, she was stunning from head to toe. Many women starved themselves in an effort to have a figure like hers and bought contacts to mimic her natural eye color. But her intelligence was just as impressive as her physical appearance. She was at the height of her career. She owned two vehicles. Every room in her house looked like one from a home décor magazine. The son she'd given away loved her to the moon and back. And her latest win: snagging Lawrence.

Venni had done everything wrong early in her life, and she was still on top. Tangela didn't think that was fair. She didn't want her sister to lose, but she wanted her to deal with some consequences. Little did she know, Venni was dealing with major consequences…internally.

They chatted a few more minutes before Venni ended the conversation to go meditate. After a long soak in the tub, she lounged in bed and watched *Sports Center* until her eyelids got heavy. It was only ten o'clock, but she needed to get some rest. Lawrence would be at her house at three so they could be on time for their five o'clock flight.

Just after she nestled her head into her pillow and pulled the comforter up to her neck, her phone vibrated on the nightstand. She slid her hand out and held the phone at arm's length. It was a text message from Vance.

```
I need to talk to u 2morrow. U were right.
Got more than the Jordan stuff from Ava.
Don't tell mom.
```

Venni shook her head. She knew it. Her baby wasn't a baby anymore. She was going to call him as soon as he got out of school to make sure he wasn't going to make any babies or catch something more than a chest-pass. She was thankful he felt comfortable discussing his newly found sex life with an adult, and it was awkwardly flattering that he chose her. There was no way he could tell Theodore or Tangela that he'd had sex. Theodore was unapproachable; and Tangela...well, most boys would rather eat glass than tell their mother that they "got some." If Vance only knew he *was* telling his mother....

CHAPTER 8

#45

"A short retirement urges a sweet return."
— John Milton

Venni joined Lawrence at the craps table. He turned to her after he placed his bet. "Did you get him?"

"Yeah," she replied.

"Everything alright?"

"He's on cloud nine. So, I suppose." She waited for the bystanders to collect their winnings and placed a bet for the next round. "He lost his virginity yesterday."

"What?!" Lawrence said with childlike excitement. "Big V got some birthday booty?"

Venni chastised him with an elbow to his ribs. Lawrence laughed more.

"Did you tell him not to get some before his game tonight?"

Venni laughed. "I wasn't even thinking about that. I was more focused on the condom conversation."

"You better text him so he won't go hit it before the game. That boy's legs will be wobbly as hell, tryin' to run down the court."

She shook her head. "I'm still trippin' that I'm even talking about sex with him."

"It's cool that he talks to you, though. Can you imagine him talkin' to Theodore?"

"Oh, God...."

Lawrence laughed. "You never know. He might be a boss in the sheets."

"Please. I'm quite confident that he's far from a boss. I doubt Tangie even takes the time to search for his barely-there dick if it isn't a holiday. She probably has five layers of dust down there; so thick, you can't even see the cobwebs."

Lawrence turned his attention away from the table to look at Venni.

She knew exactly what he was thinking. "Shut up!" she said. "I dust down there frequently. This here has never seen a cobweb."

"You should hire a cleaning service next time. Everybody deserves a break. You know I do that on the side. Right? I'll hook you up free of charge the first time."

Venni gave him a playful nudge with her forearm. "Only the first time? What's your rate after that?"

He collected his winnings and they left the table hand-in-hand. "I'd charge you a flat fee." He tapped the left side of her chest with his index finger. "I want that."

"You have it."

"Forever."

Venni smiled contemplatively and nodded.

❧

Body English was packed. The kickoff party was in full-swing. Nick Cannon was hyped, as any host should be. Energy was high. Bar tabs were skyrocketing. Half-dressed groupies were swarming. Music was loud. Bass was hitting hard enough to recalibrate heartbeats. Even in V.I.P., there wasn't much room to move. But it was All-Star weekend in Vegas, and no one cared.

Venni and Lawrence sat in a booth with Herb and some of his buddies. Herb was a former client of Lawrence's who'd first put the idea in his head to attend the weekend festivities. They popped bottles, talked shit, peeped celebrities and their dates, and bobbed their heads to the music.

Venni caught herself admiring Lawrence through the night. He was debonair in his blazer and button-down. Beyond that, he was just downright impressive. He'd whisked her away for real—and not to a cliché island so they could walk hand-in-hand on the beach. He gifted her with a trip that allowed her to watch the game she loved—the ultimate game—and she was happy to share that moment with the man she loved.

Once the liquor settled in Venni's system, she was ready to dance. She grabbed her handsome date by the hand, and they two-stepped, grinded, and got low; fitting in perfectly with those who surrounded them. Sensuality was at its peak as their bodies touched in the name of rhythm. Venni found herself holding onto Lawrence's lapels and pulling him close during a few songs. Most times, that was his cue to stop abiding by the twelve-inches rule that was enforced at most middle school dances. Other times, she used the opportunity to kiss his perfect lips.

At about 1 a.m., another quick peck turned into a much more involved makeout session. PDA wasn't Venni's thing, but she'd forgotten that anyone else was around. She was wrapped up in moment, thanking her man for an awesome Valentine's Day gift...over and over.

They stopped once a drunk groupie bumped into them. Venni spoke with her lips grazing his ear. "Let's get out of here."

"Aw, babe, don't let that girl kill our vibe." He started dancing again.

Venni leaned in again. "I'm ready to go." Her hot pants had become wet pants, and she needed to come out of them.

Lawrence glanced over at their booth. Herb and his friends looked like they weren't even close to calling it a night. Venni could see the disappointment on his face.

She tapped his shoulder. "You can stay if you want, but I have to leave before I flood the place."

Lawrence squinted. Venni looked down at her pelvis. Cleared up his confusion.

"So what you sayin'?" he asked.

"Nothin'. Wolf tickets are cheap. I told you I'm done talking."

And so was Lawrence. They returned to the booth and said their goodbyes. The men at the table winked at him before they took off. There was only one reason to rush off from a nightclub when the party was just getting started.

Luckily, they didn't have to go far. They were staying right there in the Hard Rock Hotel. They enjoyed the elevator ride alone with Venni tucked into the back corner and Lawrence pressed against her. They squeezed in as many sweet kisses as the forty-second ride allowed. "You enjoying yourself so far?" Lawrence asked.

Venni nodded and looked into his eyes. Her gaze expressed her appreciation, love, and lust. Lawrence read her loud and clear.

BOONG! They arrived at their floor and walked hand-in-hand to their suite. Lawrence took in slow, deep breaths, trying to calm his nerves. He had been ready for Venni since he met her, but she'd put him on the spot. The spontaneity of her decision to finally make love, though thrilling, gave him anxiety he hadn't felt since eleventh grade when his boys dared him to have sex with a friend's thirty-year-old aunt. Just two days prior, Venni had rejected him on the couch. Now, she was freshening up in the bathroom while he downed a glass of Crown Royal in the sitting area.

He didn't know what to do while he waited. She told him to "stay put" before she turned on some slow jams, disappeared into the bedroom, and shut the door. He sniffed his underarms. Good. Shook his hips. No sticky balls. Good. He was ready. He pulled off his blazer and flung it onto the couch. Now what? Would he look over-anxious if he took off his shirt, too? Should he at least come out of his shoes? He poured a little more Crown. Sipped. Stepped out of his shoes.

What's she doing? he thought as he sat on the sofa. He adjusted to accommodate his growing erection. Just then, Venni opened the bedroom door and leaned against the frame wearing nothing but a Michael Jordan #45 jersey that barely reached the bottom of her nether region. She nodded her head toward the room behind her.

Lawrence smiled widely and stood. "Okay, number forty-five. I see you. You're out of retirement. I like that."

He unbuttoned his shirt as he walked toward her, and she helped him out of it. He swept her hair behind her ear and kissed her from her forehead to her cheeks to her collar bones. He dropped to his knees and kissed her ankles. Moved to her calves. Lingered on her thighs.

Venni gripped the door frame as Lawrence lifted her jersey and planted three pecks on the tattoo just above her pubic region. The words, *Father, Forgive Me* stared back at him. They were beautifully written, but inspired by the most dismal time in her life. Lawrence wanted to love any residual pain away.

"I love you, Venita Miles," he said before he cupped her perfectly round gluts and pulled her closer. "All of you," he added. His breath tickled her clitoris and sent shockwaves through the piercing therein.

Venni held onto his head with her free hand as he buried his face in her middle and used his tongue to flick the tiny dangling handcuffs attached to the barbell. He skillfully navigated the space, exceeding every expectation Venni had. She'd certainly been pleasured during her sexual career, but not like this. This was different. Every sensation was heightened. She tucked her lip between her teeth in an effort to stifle her climactic sounds. He stopped just when she was about to blow.

As he rose to his feet, he scooped her into his arms and carried her to the bed. She pulled the jersey over her head while he slipped out of his jeans and boxer briefs. She enjoyed the view as he stood before her at attention. All fear and reservation was gone. She wanted this. With his eyes on her and hers on him, she slid her fingers into the awaiting crevice, taunting him as her freshly manicured nails acquired an additional gloss.

Lawrence watched for a while, stroking his hand up and down the length of his hardness. "You can't have all the fun," he said before climbing onto the bed and hovering over her. He hung just centimeters above her opening.

"Gimme that," he said, nodding toward her hand.

Like a good girl, she did as she was told; inserting her two previously occupied fingers into his mouth. Lawrence sucked them dry and lowered himself slowly until he entered her. Venni couldn't withhold the moan that escaped from her lips.

Equally affected, Lawrence quivered and stopped at the halfway point. "Gotdamn, baby. Hold up." He stopped to gather himself. Twelve months of using lotion and his imagination was no comparison to the warmth of his woman. She accommodated him well as he reached the depth of her.

Venni was overcome with hypersensitivity. This was the first time she'd voluntarily had sex without a condom. She felt every vein, every ripple of him. She'd only had battery-operated toys inside of her over the past ten years, and even though she knew there was nothing like the real thing, she wasn't prepared for toe-curling satisfaction of this magnitude. Not when they were barely getting started.

"I could stay in here all night," Lawrence said as he slowly began to move.

"What's stopping you?" Venni reciprocated his movements as they found their way to ecstasy.

"This good—"

He gripped the headboard. She dug her nails into his back. He bit the pillow. She bit his shoulder. Just when he thought he'd gone as far as he could, Venni crossed her ankles around his neck and arched her back. There, he found her spot, and she found her fireworks.

With the sensation growing stronger and stronger, she asked, "Do you feel that?"

"Yeah," Lawrence said between pants as her muscles pulsated around him. "You ready to cum for me?"

"*With* you."

She swiveled her hips. He lengthened his strokes. Within seconds, they were clenching each other and trembling, and it wasn't because they were in danger. Out of breath and depleted of energy, they lay next to each other with their bodies still intertwined.

"I can't feel my legs," Venni said.

"That's a good thing." He played with her hair. "You think they heard us next door?"

"We'll know if they call me by name in the hallway tomorrow."

"You got jokes."

"I didn't know you were a screamer, baby," she said.

"Me, neither."

They laughed. Venni snuggled against Lawrence's chest. She had never felt this. She'd had sex too many times to count, but there was no love involved. All previous orgasms were attributed to the laws of physiology. Like a reflex, if a man hit the right spot, her body reacted.

The thumps from Lawrence's heartbeat reverberated in her ear. "So this is what it feels like. Huh?" she asked as her fingers traced his ribs.

"What do you mean?"

"Love. In translation," Venni replied.

Sex began as an experiment at age thirteen, transformed into a cry for attention, evolved into an entrepreneurial endeavor, and morphed into an act of manipulation. Now at age thirty, she finally understood what it was like to make love. She felt the correlation between two bodies connecting and two hearts connecting—a fascinating parallel. Lawrence touched her like she was precious. He looked at her like she was angelic. He loved her like it was necessary. If her body could smile, it would have. It felt like it already was.

CHAPTER 9

No Excuse

*"Waiting is a trap. There will always be reasons to wait...The
truth is, there are only two things in life, reasons and results, and
reasons simply don't count."*

- Robert Anthony

Whaaaat?!" Keyonna exclaimed.

"It's about time!" Gabriella added.

They were barely ten minutes into the phone call, and already, Venni's girls didn't disappoint. She was in stitches. Kissing and telling wasn't her thing, but taking her relationship with Lawrence to the next level was worthy of reporting.

"Who initiated it?" Keyonna asked.

Venni recounted the story of her luring Lawrence from the club and changing into the Michael Jordan jersey. She explained the significance of the jersey, citing Lawrence's quip about her claiming to be the best but acting like she was retired every time he made an advance toward her.

"That...shit...was...epic," Keyonna said. "You make me wanna up my game. I feel like I'm slipping."

"Did he rip it off of you?" Gabriella asked.

"No." Venni told the rest of the story in Cliff's Notes fashion, careful not to speak too much about her boo's prowess.

"And he knows how to clean the plate?" Gabriella probed.

"So well, I'm sure he saw his reflection," Venni said.

"Yes, mami! Yes!"

"I bet it was explosive," Keyonna said with a dreamy sigh.

"'Explosive' isn't even the word," Venni replied.

Venni knew Keyonna and Gabriella would be ecstatic to hear she and Lawrence had finally had sex. The moment was much like when she told her friend Cierra that she'd lost her virginity to Roderick. This time, though, her excitement wasn't juvenile. She was engaging in grown folks' business and had grown folks' feelings.

"It took you long enough to tell us. Damn!" Gabriella said.

"I've been back from Vegas for a whopping two weeks. Calm down."

Keyonna chimed in. "She didn't have time to call us. That woman has been otherwise occupied, G. They probably screw like newlyweds now."

"Or porn stars," Gabriella added.

"Y'all are a trip," Venni said.

Keyonna was right, though. Venni craved Lawrence. They happily overdosed on pleasure when they were together. They didn't have sex every day, but it was safe to say that on many nights, their cool-downs at the gym were in vain. Once they got home, their heart rates were back up.

"Did it hurt? It's been like ten years. Right?" Gabriella asked.

"You are so damn inappropriate," Venni replied. "No, fool. It took some time for him to get all the way in, but I wasn't in pain."

Though Venni was comfortable with Lawrence, she still had her hang-ups. They even had a nonverbal signal to communicate when something was out of bounds for her—three taps to his shoulder. Lawrence already knew why she couldn't return oral favors. That story disgusted him. But there were other positions and acts that threatened to give her flashbacks of the time when having sex was part of her job description. He was sensitive to pleasing her without traumatizing her; and since she didn't want to run down her list of no-nos like she was participating in a pre-intercourse survey, their signal helped them avoid the awkwardness of her yelling, "Stop!" or worse yet, spazzing out like a maniac beneath him.

"You know he's really gonna want that ring on it now," Keyonna said.

Venni sighed. "I know."

"Has he mentioned it anymore?"

"Yeah. He talks about it jokingly, but I know he's serious. A couple days ago, he said he should propose naked this time and see what I say."

They all laughed.

"What would you say?" Gabriella asked.

"I don't know. Y'all know this love stuff was not in my plans."

"And now it is. Suck it up, cupcake."

"I hope you can see my middle finger through the phone," Venni replied.

"What would stop you from saying 'Yes' now?" Keyonna asked. "Girl, you better get you some of this married life."

❧

"Okay," Dr. Cox began. "Let's get into your 'What.'"

Venni folded one leg under her bottom, making herself comfortable. "Let's do it."

"'Torn.' Talk to me about that."

"It has to do with Lawrence. And now it's worse."

Venni admitted how in love she was with him and explained how she could see herself being with him for the long haul. In the passing month since they'd consummated their relationship in Vegas, their connection had grown stronger and she was leaning even more toward forever. Still, taking it day by day felt safer.

"I love that you're thinking about the future, but don't pressure yourself with words like 'forever,'" Dr. Cox said with a smile.

"I have an engagement ring sitting on my dresser between my Burberry perfume and my watch collection," Venni said.

"He proposed in Vegas?" Dr. Cox's tone rose an octave.

"No. Last year."

She recounted the story of Lawrence's Fourth of July proposal that took place while they were downtown watching the fireworks display. She accepted the ring, not wanting to embarrass him in front of their audience of strangers; but once they returned to her house, she slid the ring off and handed it to him.

"Apparently he didn't have hard feelings since you two are still together," Dr. Cox concluded.

"I told him it was too soon. We had just gotten together in April."

"When men are ready for marriage, there's usually a strange urgency to it."

Venni smiled. "Most definitely. I think we were already a couple in his head from the day we met, though. So in his mind, we'd been together for years." She and the doctor shared a laugh. "He told me to keep the ring because I was gonna need it later."

"Confident man."

"He knows what he wants."

"And you don't?"

"I know I love him. I know I enjoy his company. I know he makes me happy."

"But what do you want? He wants you. Do you want him?"

"He has me and I have him."

"So why not accept the ring?"

Venni threw her hand in the air and it landed in her lap with a loud smack. "I guess because the ring comes with more responsibility. It comes with me telling him the one thing I left out back in April."

"Which was…?"

"That Vance is my son."

Dr. Cox took a in a deep breath. "Okay. Let's backtrack a bit. What does he already know?"

"Everything else. He knows I found Cassidy dead. He knows where the burn marks on my back came from. He knows I've slept with over—" She caught herself. "He knows me."

"So you told him *all* about FT?" Dr. Cox asked.

Venni nodded. "Before I agreed to date him. That was important to me."

"Wow. Help me understand why you opened up to him about the things that are most sensitive to you. You're such a private person."

"It felt okay. I don't know how else to explain it. He's my best friend. He shared some very personal things with me—secrets—after we'd known each other for about year. He trusted me. It took me longer to feel the same way, but..." Her voice trailed off. "I needed him to know about my past. He knew I had PTSD, but he didn't know what traumatic events caused it. He'd seen my tattoo, but he didn't know the inspiration behind it. He knew not to ever order me a hot dog at the baseball stadium, but he didn't know why I hated them. There was no way we could be in a relationship without me filling in the blanks."

Dr. Cox nodded. "And what was his reaction?"

Venni first talked about her approach; how she looked Lawrence in the eyes the night after she told him to drop the anchorwoman and said she had to do some dirty laundry before they could move forward. She wanted terribly to have the conversation while she was sober but had to reach out to Grey Goose for some liquid courage a half hour before he came to her house. As it turned out, baring her soul was more terrifying than lying nude with strangers ever was.

"He was quiet for a while," Venni said. "He did a lot of blinking. He said 'Wow' about thirty times. He asked questions. He wanted to know when I last accepted payment for sex. He asked what types of things I had to do. I was completely transparent with him."

"And that was it? You two went on with the evening?"

Venni described the awkwardness between her and Lawrence that lasted almost a week. She'd told him about her Fast Track adventures on a Sunday. That next Thursday, he sent an oversized print of Maya Angelou's 'Phenomenal Woman' poem—custom framed—to her office with a note that simply read, "Honesty is worthy of respect. Respect is the foundation of love. I didn't know I could love or respect you more until last Sunday. Thank you for giving me that part of you. – L"

"For me, that was confirmation that telling him was okay."

"So why did you leave out the part about Vance?"

"Because I don't feel he should know if Vance doesn't know."

For the first time in the session, Dr. Cox jotted down a quick note. "Will Vance ever know?"

"Vance has a mother who loves him and an aunt who loves him more. He knows that."

Dr. Cox stared at Venni with her brow slightly furrowed.

Venni continued. "It's almost a catch twenty-two. I won't marry Lawrence while I'm holding on to this secret. The secret will remain a secret until Tangie or I tell Vance, because he deserves to know his truth before an outsider does. The problem is I have no intention of telling him I'm his mother. So, here I am. Torn."

"So what are you going to do? If you've made up your mind that you're not going to tell Vance the truth, why stay in the relationship with Lawrence?"

"Dr. Cox, if my thoughts made sense, if I knew the answer to that, I wouldn't be here."

She studied Venni's eyes at length. "Is there something I'm missing here?"

There was. Venni was holding back a little. She didn't tell the doctor how Lawrence spoke openly and regularly about wanting a son and gushed about how great of a mother she would be since she was a natural with Vance. She wondered if that was the type of "something" the doctor was referring to.

She felt more and more transparent the longer Dr. Cox looked at her.

"Lawrence wants a son," she said softly. "He talks about how we'd be as first-time parents. And I let him." Despondency and fear translated through her eyes.

Dr. Cox now had a better understanding of what was really going on. Venni had missed opportunities to tell Lawrence that she was already a mother, and she didn't know how to go back and right her wrong. Better yet, she'd realized there was no way to "fix" it. She'd simply have to own up to her lie and risk losing Lawrence's trust. Either way, she had to be more realistic about her motives or lack thereof.

Dr. Cox's timer vibrated in her pants pocket. She set her pen and notepad on the table beside her. "You know, sometimes we set rules for ourselves that do more harm than good; and we forget that we can break those rules. Lawrence sounds like a sweet guy who is undoubtedly in love. Have faith in him. That's all I will say."

Venni raised an eyebrow. "Are you this optimistic with everybody?"

"When warranted. Venni, I know there may be some men who appreciate a woman's honesty, but I bet the list of men who stick around after hearing the things you've already told Lawrence could fit on a Post-It note. I understand where your hesitance stems from in this situation, but make sure Vance is your reason—not your excuse."

CHAPTER 10

Mom?

"Our life is composed greatly from dreams, from the unconscious, and they must be brought into connection with action. They must be woven together."

— Anais Nin

Venni sat straight up in bed. She looked right and left, but saw nothing but darkness. In her dream, she was at the grocery store perusing the various brands of spaghetti sauce. They were out of Prego, and she didn't want Ragu. She was pissed. A nearby shopper told her a manager would be right with her. So, she stood with her arms crossed and waited.

It felt real. She felt the tap on her shoulder. Saw the plum nail polish. Smelled Estée Lauder perfume. When she turned around, her mother, Rita, was standing within a foot of her, wearing her favorite wig—the one she had custom made after her cancer diagnosis, the one she said she wore when she was feeling "cute." And Venni heard her voice as clear as day.

"It's time." Stern and matter-of-fact, her mother's words resounded even after she awoke.

Venni failed at steadying her trembling hands. She was feeling a hodgepodge of emotions. Her mother had appeared in her dreams regularly postmortem. In high school, if Venni dreamed she was at a movie theater, her mother would be seated a few rows in front of her. If she dreamed she was in a crowded elevator, her mother would make eye contact with her and turn away. There was always sadness in her eyes, though.

In fact, the first time Rita smiled at Venni was when she dreamed that she and Lawrence were walking down a deserted country road after running out of gas. When they reached the station, her mother was pumping gas and grinned as they walked by. And that dream took place after she and Lawrence had become a couple. The more she thought about it, her mother had been smiling ever since. But she'd never said a word. Ever. Until now.

Hearing her mother's voice was like drinking Gatorade after a five mile run—refreshing. For years, she'd recognized her mother's presence in her dreams as reassurance that she would always be with her. Even though Rita usually cut her eyes at her wayward daughter or shook her head with disappointment, Venni didn't mind. "Seeing" her around was never a bad thing.

But this time, she spoke. What did she mean? It was time for what? To speak to her in her dreams? She tried to fall asleep again quickly in hopes of continuing the dream. Unfortunately, she dreamed of going to the children's museum with some random baby girl she was pushing in a stroller. She awoke the next morning, wondering if her mother meant it was time for her to have another child.

Was she pregnant? She took her birth control pill at the same time every day, but many women were known to still get pregnant while using the contraceptive. She couldn't be pregnant, though. Right? Well, technically, she could be. But the universe wouldn't do that to her. The timing was totally off. By the time she showered and toweled off, she'd convinced herself that she was letting her imagination run rampant. She shook off that thought. She wasn't pregnant. No way.

Two nights later, her mother appeared again. This time, she sat next to her at one of Vance's basketball games. When he stood at the free throw line to take his foul shots, she turned to Venni.

"You need to tell him." She turned her attention back to the basketball court and cheered Vance on.

"Tell him what?" Venni asked aloud as she broke from Lawrence's hold and sat up in bed.

Lawrence sat up, too, alarmed. "What's wrong?"

"Nothing," Venni lied. "I guess I was just having a bad dream."

"About?"

Venni lay back down. She reached behind her and grabbed Lawrence's hand. He followed her lead, positioning his body against hers and hooking his arm around her again. Kissed the back of her head. "I fight monsters. Just say the word."

"Oh, so you do it all. Huh?"

"And then some."

They chuckled, and soon Lawrence was fast asleep again. Venni lay with her eyes closed, but she was still awake. She wondered if her subconscious was running wild after the previous week's session with Dr. Cox. They'd talked so much about her being torn; about whether she should tell Lawrence about Vance. There was no other logical reason for this topic suddenly incorporating itself into her dream sequences after sixteen years. Perhaps her subconscious was trying to sort things out for her through her dreams. The trouble was she didn't ask for any assistance.

"*You need to tell him.*" She heard her mother's voice over and over the next day at work. There was no need for Vance to know about her unconventional part-time job in high school. So, the only thing she *needed* to tell him was the truth about their biological relationship. Why?

Her mother had sixteen years to say something. Instead, she used the time to only make cameos that conveyed her disappointment. A part of Venni resented her for creating this pothole on her road to nirvana.

The more she thought about it, the more the first dream made sense. Vance loved her lasagna, and that must have been why she needed the Prego. She remembered holding a box of noodles in her hand. She remembered fussing to the stranger in the aisle about not having time for "this shit" because "he" was coming in two hours. And then her mother appeared. It was all coming back.

She started to tell Dr. Cox during their session that evening, but ultimately opted out of sharing. The quicker they could move on from discussing why she was torn, the quicker the dreams would stop. At least that sounded logical.

She had a week of reprieve. Not only had Rita stopped talking, she stopped appearing in her dreams. Venni was convinced that ignoring her mother had worked. However, she soon discovered that what didn't work in real life didn't work in her dream world, either. On Wednesday, Rita was back.

"Tell Vance the truth, Venni Mini. Move forward. This is bigger than you." She held Venni's hand this time. They were working at what looked to be a soup kitchen, stocking shelves with canned goods. "Keep on," she warned, "you can sugarcoat the truth, but it eventually wears off to its raw and bitter core."

Hearing the pet name her mother gave her at the age of three shocked her soul. She found comfort in the words, but they also summoned old feelings that made her miss her mother as much as she did when she first passed away. And her advice was reminiscent of the clever guidance she offered when Venni and her first best friend "broke up" in the sixth grade. Confusion had set in again. Why was her mother pressing this issue now?

⚬⚬⚬

Lawrence pulled his shirt over his head as Venni exited the bathroom. "Hey, pretty girl," he greeted before he planted a kiss on her forehead.

She finished drying off the excess water from the shower. "I thought you would've been gone by now," Venni said.

"I'm on my way out. I just wanted to make sure you were cool."

"Why wouldn't I be?" She flashed her best smile.

"You didn't wake up last night, baby, but you tossed and turned for like twenty minutes. What are you dreaming about? Have you talked to Dr. Cox about this yet?"

"Lawrence, I'm fine."

"You're not."

"You can't tell me how I feel."

"Why won't you at least share what's happening in the dreams with me? Is it me? Is this your PTSD messing with you? Am I doing something to stir it up?"

"No," Venni said. She stood and held his hands. "You're doing everything right, baby. I'll be okay. It'll pass."

Lawrence wanted to believe her, but he didn't even know what "it" was. As much as Venni tried to shrug off the dreams, they affected her. And since they affected her, they affected him. He understood that he couldn't stop the occurrences, but he was willing to try his best to help her ward off the demons that seemed to torture her while she slept. With their anniversary coming up that weekend, he was hoping "it" would "pass" sooner than later.

His fear was that Venni's choice to make love with him was backfiring. Maybe her body was ready, but her mind was not. Even though she wasn't the type of woman who could be pressured into doing something she didn't want to do, he couldn't help but wonder if she'd jumped the gun in Vegas. Or maybe their bountiful sex life was subliminally reminding her of her past and the memories manifested in her dreams. Whatever the trigger, Venni was stubborn enough to think she could overcome such torment on her own. She was stubborn enough to keep "it" to herself.

Lawrence stared into her gorgeous eyes. "Don't shut me out. Okay?"

She tilted her head back and puckered her lips. Lawrence leaned down to get a taste. "You better get outta here before I take advantage of you," Venni said before she cupped the bulge in his warm-up pants.

He smacked her bare behind and kissed her again on her forehead. "Make sure you call the lady to see if we can check in early on Friday," he said before he left.

"Make sure *you* get to work before Mrs. Anderson cusses you out," Venni replied. "I know what I need to take care of, Mr. Blackwell."

That Friday at noon, she and Lawrence received their room keys for their anniversary getaway. Instead of going on a cruise or flying to an island, they opted to stay at a luxury ranch resort within driving distance. It was perfect. Low-key and ideal for much-needed relaxation, they welcomed the time away from highly populated tourist spots.

While Venni enjoyed time at the spa, Lawrence went fishing. They went horseback riding, skinny-dipped in the private pool, walked the trails, shot pool.... All three nights, they lay on blankets and stargazed on the lawn in front of the lodge. They celebrated happiness. They celebrated life...with each other. When Venni showed Camden the brochure upon her return to work, he summed up their vacation by saying they did "white people stuff." Whether the "stuff" was for white, black, red, or green people, she was happy to have done it with her man. Best of all, she didn't have any of the "Tell Vance" dreams.

Months prior, Dr. Cox told her she had gotten to the good part and hadn't realized it. She didn't believe her. But since then, she'd gained panoramic perspective. Since the old saying warned that all good things come to an end, Venni wanted to ask Dr. Cox a follow-up question: Could she press pause?

CHAPTER 11

Shutout

*"Right actions in the future are the best
apologies for bad actions in the past."*

— Tryon Edwards

Venni and Dr. Cox used the first few minutes of their
session to catch up. Venni told her about the anniversary
trip and how much fun she and Lawrence had.

Dr. Cox noted that Venni didn't say she told Lawrence
about Vance. They'd spent several sessions considering the
topic, but apparently she still wasn't ready. Dr. Cox knew that
a romantic getaway wasn't the ideal time to bring up such
heavy information; but something told her that until Venni
recognized there was never a good moment to tell such major
news, Lawrence would remain in the dark. Not wanting to
press the issue, the doctor skimmed through her notes. It was
time to move on.

"What happened in 1991?" she asked.

Venni's mind was elsewhere. She stared at her favorite
spot on the wall behind the doctor and cracked her knuckles.
Thought that maybe she should ask Dr. Cox for her thoughts
on the dreams since she'd just had another one the night before.

"Are you with me today?" Dr. Cox asked.

Venni returned her focus to Dr. Cox. "Yes. I'm sorry."

"Is there something you want to talk about first?" She shook her head. "Vance happened in 1991. I became a mother."

"So that's your 'when.' Why did you pick that year?"

"Because I feel like I'm stuck there. I'm not still rocking oversized overalls and Hi-Tech boots, but my secrets are."

Dr. Cox chuckled a bit. "You just made me remember some of my nineties wardrobe. I get it."

Venni chuckled, too.

"I love that metaphor. Not only are those secrets covered, they're covered well, in unassuming clothing," Dr. Cox said. Venni nodded in response. "So what do you need to move forward? How do we get you to 2007?"

"I guess I need to tell Lawrence and Vance about 1991. It's that simple."

"Is that the year you witnessed the murder also?"

"Nah," Venni replied.

"What about the burns?"

Venni shook her head. "That stuff happened later. That's when adventure turned to danger and I got the hell outta there." Silence. "But I guess a part of me will always remain in the nineties."

"Why?"

"Once you see blood pouring from someone's body and their eyes rolled back, you're never the same."

"And you actually saw the person kill her," Dr. Cox stated. She'd wanted clarification on this since Venni vaguely mentioned it in their first session.

"Yeah, from afar."

"And she was in FT also?"

Venni cut her eyes in the doctor's direction. "Yeah, but the guy who killed her wasn't a part of FT. FT was a controlled environment."

Dr. Cox noticed Venni's clenched jaw and balled fist. "How did you get the burns?" she asked, hoping that a change of topic would prevent Venni's foreseeable shutdown.

Venni shifted on the couch. "From a cigar." She rolled her eyes. "A blunt."

"Someone burned you with their cigar? Purposely? Repeatedly? Why?"

"I don't think assholes need reasons." She stood and removed her suit jacket. Turned so her back was facing the doctor. "Go ahead," she said.

Dr. Cox stood and held the bottom of Venni's cami between her fingers. She lifted the garment slowly, revealing eight round scars that lined Venni's spine. The darkened circles looked to have healed well, but their presence was disturbing.

"Add that to why I'll always be stuck in the nineties. All the Mederma in the world can't take away the scars."

"Honestly, they aren't that bad," Dr. Cox said. She ran her finger across the only raised scar.

"I'm not talking about those."

Dr. Cox released Venni's cami and the ladies returned to their seats. "You're healing, Venni. I see it. You don't feel it?"

"I've noticed changes. You've helped me understand some of my behaviors and actions. At the end of the day, though…" Venni couldn't find the words to finish her thought.

"It's a process," Dr. Cox reminded.

"Well, my process looks like it's gonna affect the two people I love. A part of me wishes I never started the process."

"Do you mean that?"

Venni looked away.

"I never told you this would be easy," Dr. Cox said.

"I don't like the idea of my baggage becoming an unexpected burden on someone else."

"So don't let it. We all have baggage, and that's okay. Knowing how to pack light is the key. We often hold on to things that can be left behind. Our pasts have happened. There's no erasing them. Setting some of the heavy stuff aside doesn't mean you're ignoring it; it just means you're not carrying it with you. I follow the rules of most airlines. If it can't fit under the seat in front of me or in the overhead compartment, it can't travel with me. You have to get rid of what's weighing you down, Venni."

Venni was quiet for a few seconds. "Do you believe that dreams and reality can mesh?"

"I'm not sure what you're asking."

"Let me back up. I think I told you during our first month about my mom randomly being in my dreams ever since she died."

"Right. We discussed how she always looked at you like she was upset or disappointed."

"Yeah. Until I got with Lawrence."

Dr. Cox nodded. "Once you found happiness, her happiness returned."

"Now, she's talking." Venni told the doctor about each dream she'd had. Dr. Cox listened intently. "She wasn't in any of my dreams during our trip, but yesterday, she showed up again, pointing to a calendar. June," Venni continued.

"Can you think of any significance of that month?"

"Just that Vance is coming to stay with me for a few weeks. Do you think she's implying that I should tell him when he comes?"

Dr. Cox shrugged slowly.

"He comes every year, though. I can't figure out why she's talking to me now and why telling Vance the truth is the only thing she's talking about."

"There are two things I'm confident about after hearing this, but I want you to understand that my interpretation isn't based on text from a psychology book. I'm not a dream analyst. I can tell you what I feel, what my gut says," Dr. Cox began.

"I'm all ears."

"One: She found it safe to speak to you now. Now that you're opening your heart, maybe she knew you would be more receptive to what she has to say. She's already communicated with you nonverbally—the tears during your high school years and the somber facial expressions thereafter. I won't deny you were wise beyond your years back then, but we both know you weren't intuitively mature. Or even if you were, who would you have talked this over with? From what you've told me, you barely shared anything with Holly and G, and they were your friends. You weren't ready. Now, you are.

"Two: Your mother is probably the only person you'll listen to when it comes to making this decision. We've gone round and round about this for what…a month now? I think Mom knew I needed backup." She smiled.

Venni nodded. "I guess you're right."

"You have to forgive yourself, Venni. You were young. His father took advantage of you. You did what made sense at the time."

"Are those reasons or excuses?" Venni asked meekly.

"We both know that answer," Dr. Cox replied.

Though it was apparent that Venni's soul was weeping, her eyes wouldn't. She was so hard. Dr. Cox wished she could hug her. Maybe then she'd be able to squeeze out the pain Venni wouldn't release.

Instead, she leaned forward. "You can do this. Once you forgive yourself, it won't be so unbelievable that someone else can forgive you, too. Let's get those secrets out of those overalls. Yes?"

Venni nodded.

"How was therapy?" Lawrence asked as soon as Venni walked into the kitchen.

She set her keys on the counter and sifted through the mail. "Good."

Lawrence stared at her, waiting for more. Venni ignored his gaze and opened an envelope.

"Did you finally tell her?" Lawrence continued.

Venni glanced at him, delivering a nonverbal cease and desist order.

"Venni, you can't expect me to sleep next to you and not ask questions when you wake up shaking and looking like you've seen a ghost. Tell me something!"

Venni dropped the envelope from her hands. "No offense, babe, but what can you do? If I tell you, what can you do about it?"

Lawrence took a gulp of his water and huffed with frustration. "I guess nothing." He walked out of the room and went to his favorite spot in her house—the den.

He was over Venni and her avoidance tactics. He'd tried being patient, understanding, cautious with his questioning... all that. His only other alternative was to be aggressive, and he knew that would only piss her off. But he was peeved, too. What bothered him most was she was willing to hold on to her dream-secret at the expense of alienating him. He'd planned on staying the night, but the more he thought about it, the better sleeping in his own bed sounded.

After they said their goodbyes, Venni changed into her running gear. It was still daylight, so she had time to squeeze in at least three miles. She needed it. She needed her endorphins to flood her body with "feel-good" and make her forget about her worries...even if it was temporary. The sounds of The Black Eyed Peas blasted through her ear buds, but all she heard was Dr. Cox. *"You have to forgive yourself...You have to get rid of what's weighing you down, Venni."*

Once she made it back home, she soaked in the tub and found comfort in the scent of jasmine. She rendezvoused with her thoughts until the water cooled off, ultimately making peace with herself. Before she went to bed, she texted Lawrence.

```
I know you're probably still
pissed, but I wanted to say
I luv u before I hit these
sheets. I'm sorry about earlier.
I'm working on it. Hope u still
have some patience left.
```

CHAPTER 12

This is Why

"Most quarrels amplify a misunderstanding."

– Andre Gide

Lawrence was quiet during dinner. Venni knew what was bothering him. He was still mad from their mini argument two days prior. She tried to remain positive and upbeat, knowing she was responsible for his disposition.

"What are we doing this weekend?" she asked.

Lawrence shrugged and finished chewing.

"Do you feel like going to Branson's beach house? Remember he invited us for his pre-birthday bash," Venni continued. "I would only make an appearance because he's my boss and I feel obligated. You know?"

"That's Saturday?" Lawrence replied without looking up from his plate.

"Yeah. Camden's crazy ass is going. You know he'll keep it exciting." Venni found that she was the only one laughing.

In response to Lawrence's grunt of disinterest, Venni took a drink of her lemonade and cleared her throat. "I turned down your proposal because you can't marry a woman you don't know." She rested her fork on the side of her plate and stared at it. After taking a deep breath, she looked up at Lawrence. "I don't want you to love me in pieces. You need to know the whole of me, who I really am."

"Okay…I proposed way back in July, though. I'm up for hearing why you said 'no,' but you already said it was because you wanted to get used to just being in a relationship before we made the ultimate commitment." He laughed uncomfortably. "You're kinda scaring me. What else is there to know? You've told me about Lakeside Prep. We've talked about your relationship with your parents…."

His voice trailed off. The only deal-breaker he could imagine was a Maury-Povich-like revelation that his love was once a man. But that couldn't have been. He'd seen her, felt her. A doctor couldn't have reconstructed that.

Venni didn't let Lawrence wrestle with his thoughts for long. "Vance is my son," she said with nervous pride.

Lawrence choked on his saliva, mid-swallow. Venni sat back in her chair and waited for him to recover. After a few gulps of water, Lawrence was able to speak.

"Your son?"

"I was fourteen, incapable and disgusted. Tangie was barren and willing."

"Disgusted? So you got pregnant by one of your…?"

"Something like that."

Lawrence leaned forward with his forearms resting on the table. "No. We're not doing half-answers. Do you even know who his father is?"

Venni hadn't prepared for that question, so it stung. Though she'd be labeled a ho in most people's books, Lawrence knew the context of her licentious lifestyle. Unconventional? Yes. Unmanaged? No. "His father is my high school principal. He was a part of the Fast Track operation. He liked stray cats, but he *loved* mine. His wife couldn't have children. I could. And apparently in his native land, grown men sexing adolescents was normal. Whole answer."

"Did he rape you?"

"If we get technical, men made appointments to rape me for four years."

Lawrence clenched his jaw and breathed slowly out of his nostrils. "Native land? So his uncle that he visits in Chicago—"

"Hassan is his father, not his uncle." Venni confirmed.

"Vance has his eyebrows. He looks like your dad, though. *You* look like your dad." Lawrence shared his thoughts aloud as he put the pieces together. "He's just like you. Personality, athleticism…everything. Now you buying the car makes sense."

"I haven't been sleeping because of my mom. She keeps visiting me in my dreams, and she's telling me that Vance needs to know the truth. I'm starting to think—"

Lawrence pushed back from the table and stood up. "I gotta get outta here. We'll talk later."

He wiped his mouth with the napkin and threw it in the middle of the plate on top of his barely-eaten meal. Venni cocked her head to the side as he exited the kitchen and walked into the foyer. She watched him snatch his jacket from the coat rack and yank open the door. Though the words he mumbled on his way out were unintelligible, his shaking head gave her the impression that he was annoyed; fed up, even.

She didn't expect complete acceptance. All of her baggage fell into the "oversized" category and was a lot to take on.

Lawrence had already piled her Lakeside Prep past onto his back, and that was more than enough for a man to carry. She had probably sexed more partners than he. Still, he loved her past her promiscuity. She got that. She appreciated that. However, she never would've guessed he'd walk out on her before they talked things over. He didn't walk out on her when she dropped her other bombs on him. She was a realist, though. Everyone had their "straw," and perhaps this bale of hay broke Lawrence's back.

There was no use in picking at her food. Lawrence had taken her appetite with him. She scraped both of their plates and set them in the sink. Transferred the remaining food from the pots to plastic containers and placed them in the refrigerator. Looked at the sink full of dishes. Shook her head and kept walking.

She ended up in her room, where she lay in bed flipping through channels. Nothing on TV piqued her interest, but she was trying to take her mind off of the knot in her stomach and the ache from her bruised heart. It didn't work. She was sick. Lawrence was her sounding board, her best friend, her "person," her man. But he walked out in the middle of the second hardest conversation she'd ever had or in this case, tried to have.

She hated that she cared. This was why she didn't get close to people. This was why she didn't love. All love had ever done was break her heart—and not always in the typical sense. Yes, she had a puppy love for her first boyfriend when she was thirteen, and he moved to a different state. Other than that, her heartache came from her mother's death, her father's disownment, and her brother's dream-chasing that landed him in LA. Everyone she'd ever loved had left her in some way. As close as she was to Gabriella and Keyonna, she wouldn't allow herself to engage in weekly catch-up phone calls or daily emails. She didn't join Connect.com to keep up with the intricate details of their lives. They kept in touch regularly, but not to the point where she looked forward to Wednesday nights at nine. This was why.

Lawrence could've at least hung around to let her know how he was feeling. She considered texting him a simple WTF? or calling to get an immediate response, but her fear of rejection acted like a force field around her phone. What if he didn't answer her call? What if he didn't text her back? He always texted her back, even when they had little arguments. But this was different. He was different. He walked out on her before an argument could ensue.

No. She wasn't going to set herself up for rejection. That was foolish girl-shit that she never partook in. She was too cool for that, too independent for that, and secretly too fragile for that.

And so the night went on. More channel-surfing. Glancing at the clock every twenty minutes. Checking her phone to make sure it wasn't on silent. Tossing and turning in bed. Hurting by accident. Hanging in the balance. After three hours, she put her heart on punishment. She'd given it an inch, and it took a mile. Lawrence should've remained in the friend zone where it was safe, where they were safe. Now Venni was unsure whether she wanted him as a friend. If Gabriella or Keyonna ever left in the middle of a conversation the way he did, she would delete them from her life without hesitation *and* empty the recycle bin. Lawrence didn't get a pass just because he shared a bed with her.

Enough. Contemplation was too complicated. She turned off her phone and the television. Set her alarm, but turned the clock radio around so that she couldn't see the display. Holding on proved to be unhealthy in the past. It was easier to let go.

She'd finally drifted off to sleep, but she was suddenly awakened by a hand resting on her shoulder. Lawrence leaned over and kissed her cheek. "I'm back, baby."

Venni looked over her shoulder to see him sitting in bed beside her. He unzipped his Nike jacket and pulled off his sneakers. She squinted with confusion, wondering if she was dreaming. Surely he wasn't climbing into bed like everything was cool. When he stood to take off his pants, she sat up.

"We can talk in the morning if you want, babe. I know it's late. I didn't think I'd be out that long. I just wanted you to know I was here," he continued.

He leaned over to give her another kiss, but she avoided it with a Matrix-like lean. "Why are you here? You have a house."

Lawrence frowned. "Whoa. What's that about?"

"I don't have shit to say to you—nothing you wanna hear—and you don't have shit to say to me. Why are you here?"

"Woman, I called and left two messages letting you know I was taking a drive and wanted to talk when I got back. I thought you didn't answer because you were asleep. I'm here 'cause I wanna be."

"Oh, now you wanna be here." She pushed the covers off and walked over to her dresser where she leaned with her arms folded.

"I didn't come back for an argument. Do I want to continue our conversation? Yes."

"You don't get to leave me, dig your panties out of your ass, and then come back expecting a civil conversation."

Lawrence walked in her direction. "You dropped another major bomb on me, V! Suddenly my lady has a teenage son. This morning, you had a teenage nephew. How was I supposed to react?"

"You're a grown man. You can react however you see fit. And you did. Instead of sticking around to talk, you bounced."

"I'ma keep it real. You didn't want to talk to me in that moment," Lawrence said. "I had sense enough to take a drive and gather my thoughts."

"This house is big enough for you to gather your thoughts without me being a hindrance. I'm a big girl. I know that news wasn't easy to swallow. But you left me. I was trying to tell you what my mom said in my dreams, and you left me." She quickly wiped the tears that streamed down her cheeks.

Lawrence was shocked to see Venni crying. She didn't cry when she told him her father died a few years prior or when she talked about Fast Track. He reached out to wipe her face, but his hand met hers.

"I'm good," Venni said, blocking his attempt at affection.

Lawrence gripped her forearm and wiped her new tears with his free hand. Venni didn't shy away from his touch. "I didn't even hear you mention your mother, baby. My head was spinning. I'm sorry. You know I wouldn't have—"

"But you did."

He took a deep breath. "I know this is a sensitive subject for you. I understand that, baby. But I have feelings, too. I think you forget that sometimes." He slid his hand down her arm and held her hand. "You're emotional. So am I. This is deep. But I'm here. Let's talk about this. What did your mom say in your dream?"

Venni looked into his eyes. There was no question he was sincere, but she was done. She took a few steps backward, pulling from Lawrence's grasp. "I don't cry," she declared as more tears dropped.

"I know. That's—"

"You were supposed to be different, but you did the same thing everybody else did. You left me. I loved you, and I was okay with it. And you left me."

"Stop saying that! I didn't leave you. I left the house. I needed some time to think."

"Then you should've stayed gone." She wiped her last tear.

"Word?"

"I'm goin' back to sleep," Venni said before she strolled to her bed.

Lawrence watched her in disbelief. He was used to her being stubborn, but she had never been cold toward him. "So I guess you don't want me here."

Deaf to his words, Venni pulled the covers over her head and turned her back to him.

CHAPTER 13

Walk Away

"If you love someone, set them free. If they come back,
they're yours; if they don't they never were."

– Richard Bach

There was a knock at the door at 11:47. Venni couldn't acknowledge it because she was on a call. Lawrence cracked her office door and stuck his head in. She finished her conversation as he stepped inside and sat across from her.

"No matter how you rephrase it, that's still unacceptable, Mr. Davenport. Why don't you take the next two days to go over your numbers again, and we'll try this negotiation... again. If we can't come to an agreement, I'll be forced to use the other vendor." Click.

"Damn!" Lawrence said. "Is that the same guy you—"

"What do you need?"

"Down, girl. I'm here to take you to lunch." He stood and pulled his keys from his pocket. "Let's go."

"I'm not hungry."

"If that's true, that's fine. I mainly want to talk."

"There's nothing to discuss, Lawrence." She arranged items on her desk that didn't need to be arranged.

Lawrence took notice. "Wow. You already got rid of our picture? It's been a week. Out of sight, out of mind?"

Venni looked at him coldly.

"I appreciate your efforts to erase me from your life, but rejecting my lunch date and tossing our picture won't change how I feel or how you feel. I'll give you more time to cool off, but you can't get rid of me that easily. We have history. You were my girl before you were my lady. We were friends. This goes beyond the bedroom…or the living room or the kitchen or the car." He smirked as he recalled the various places they'd made love. "You get my point."

Beneath her desk, Venni's leg shook with nervous energy.

"Babe, we just celebrated our anniversary ten days ago. Don't act like this. I messed up. Okay? I didn't know that going for a drive would affect you the way it did. I'm sorry. If I could drive backwards around the city to reset my odometer, I would. I'm offering to take you to lunch so we can talk, and I'm offering my undivided attention because that's all I've got. Shit, from here on out, you can hide my keys if you have something major to tell me."

Venni huffed and shook her head.

"But you don't have anything else to tell me. Right?" He smiled.

"Goodbye, Lawrence."

They stared at each other for a few uncomfortable seconds. "Alright, V. Miles." Lawrence sighed. "You're lucky I didn't tune up before I came." He tapped his neck, just above his Adam's apple. "I'd be singing Jennifer Holliday on my way out."

Though she thought his threat to sing was hilarious, Venni wouldn't allow herself to laugh.

Without looking back, he said, "I'll holla at you later, mean girl."

⁂

Venni had avoided the gym and Lawrence for three and a half weeks. Working out at home was still effective, but she missed the motivation of seeing thirty or forty other people in her vicinity who were working toward the same goal: wellness. Since Lawrence hadn't reached out to her in four days, she figured he'd finally accepted the breakup. She figured it was safe to return to the place she loved.

The warm, May breeze whipped her ponytail in all directions as she pulled her duffle bag from her trunk. She flung it onto her shoulder and looked to her right. As she expected, Lawrence's Range Rover was parked among the other employees' cars, in the seventh spot from the door. She took a deep breath and strolled to the glass doors. Before she could open one of them, Cheyenne, the girl who worked the front desk, grinned and waved with enthusiasm. Cheyenne was sweet, but sometimes she talked too damn much. Venni fought the urge to roll her eyes as she entered.

"Where have you been?" Cheyenne asked.

"I've been around. Sometimes you have to make yourself scarce so people can have the chance to miss you," Venni replied with a wink.

"Well, I know someone who definitely missed you." She nodded toward Lawrence's office.

Venni didn't look over her shoulder. Cheyenne pulled a medium-sized manila envelope from a nearby drawer. "He put this up here the other day and told us to give it to you if you came in." She changed her voice to a whisper. "It's pretty obvious that there's a CD in there, but Robin thinks there's a key inside, too. She saw him take one off of his key ring before he put the envelope up here."

"I'm glad I'm not big on surprises."

"Oh!" She covered her mouth with her hands. "I'm so sorry! I think I've just been so excited and we've been waiting for you to come in so you could get the package. Robin and I love you two. We've planned you guys' wedding in our heads and everything. You know getting a key is the first step!"

Cheyenne was unsure why she was smiling and Venni wasn't. Any woman who was in love longed for the moment she received a key to her man's house. Little did she know, Venni had a key long before she and Lawrence were a "thing." No, that wasn't a key to his house in the envelope. It was the key to hers.

Venni thanked Cheyenne and headed to the locker room. She and Lawrence caught eyes as he instructed a petite, middle-aged woman on how to use the elliptical machine. To Venni's surprise, he didn't smile or give her a head-nod-hello. He didn't give her a dirty look or abruptly cut his eyes away. He simply returned his attention to his client and continued his tutorial.

That was just the reaction Venni had hoped for. It was the reaction that made her return to the gym stress-free. After she changed clothes, she ran a half mile to warm up and went through her usual upper body workout like she did any other Friday. When she finished, she felt rejuvenated, but not like before. Her energy was off. She planned to see if her waiting bottle of wine would balance it some.

"I didn't think you were coming back."

Venni closed her trunk and turned around. Lawrence slowed his casual stroll but remained near the next row of cars. "Cheyenne gave me the envelope," she said, briefly flashing it for him to see.

"Cool. Be safe gettin' home," he said.

"You, too. And thank you. The flowers were pretty. The note was…all of it was sweet." Her words came out as awkwardly as she felt.

"It's all good." Lawrence continued the walk to his car at normal speed.

"Oh, wait!"

He stopped and walked toward her. "What's up?"

Venni struggled to work a key off of her key ring. "Before I forget…"

"I don't want that. If you don't want it, throw it away."

She stopped piddling with the keys. "I won't throw it away. I can put it with some of your other things and mail them or bring them here. Just let me know."

"I gave your key back because you had a problem with me being in your house Monday, not because I wanted mine in return. Don't play me like I'm that guy."

Venni could hear the hurt in his voice. On the Monday he was referencing, he'd entered her home while she was at work and planted a surprise for her. She was a bit cruel when she called Monday evening and asked, "Why the hell were you in my house?" instead of thanking him for the gorgeous flowers arranged around a #1 Mom balloon—a belated Mother's Day gift. He had even written a note encouraging her to proudly tell Vance she is his mother. In it, he offered to help facilitate the conversation in any way.

Lawrence's heart was huge, and he wore it on his sleeve. She could've selected more tactful words. She could've at least acknowledged his gesture. But she was caught off-guard and tired from a treacherous day at work. And still trying her best to push him away.

"What's on the CD?"

"Something I want you to listen to. It'll take less than ten minutes of your time."

Venni sighed loudly. "Lawrence…."

He stepped closer to her. "You won't answer my calls, so I stopped calling. You barely talk to me in-person. I wrote you, and I got cussed out for leaving the note inside your house. All I want you to do is listen. The lyrics in the songs say what you won't let me. You don't even have to respond." Venni shifted her weight and looked at her toes. "I understand that you're not used to being loved and I'm trying to show you what real love is; but you're turning your back on me like I never meant anything to you. I don't beat dead horses. I'm willing to fight for you, but I'm not gonna shadowbox. If you really want me to walk away, say the word."

Venni listened with the inside of her cheek clamped between her teeth. The more pressure she applied, the easier it was to focus on that pain instead of the ache in her heart.

"What's it gon' be, V. Miles?" Lawrence asked.

"I thought I made myself clear before." Venni spoke softly. She looked into his eyes. "Walk away."

Lawrence could see she didn't mean it, and it broke his heart. She was stubborn by nature, but to be outright resistant to letting him back in crushed him. There was no doubt he wanted to spend the rest of his life with her and love her through her intricacies. But she wouldn't let him. He nodded. Started to speak. Didn't see the point. Instead, he patted the roof of her BMW and granted her request.

Venni watched as he strolled away with his hands in his pockets. It was better this way. Lawrence deserved a woman who didn't need to be tutored on matters of the heart. And she deserved to return to her bubble where she rationed out her emotions in small portions, where she was safe. Besides, she never claimed she was ready for love. She'd slipped and fallen—hard. And instead of hopping right up and moving along, she stayed there. She'd reached the point now where she was done laughing at herself to cover up her embarrassment. She was now feeling the bruises, and icing her heart was her way of treating the pain.

Lawrence never looked back, and she wasn't sure whether she was proud of him or pissed at him. Before he reached his car, she entered hers and wiped a tear. She hadn't cried this much since her mother died.

She tossed the envelope onto the passenger seat and checked her rearview mirror. Clear. Off she went. That would be the last time she attended that facility. Even though Lawrence vowed to leave her alone if she asked him to, she knew it was best for both of them if she avoided the place where they'd shared so many memories.

She had already done her research. Now was the time to implement it. In approximately twenty minutes, she'd be at Clutch Sports to officially sign up for their kickboxing boot camp. "Out of sight, out of mind" typically worked for her. It was time to purge Lawrence from her system.

CHAPTER 14

Behind the Shades

"No person is your friend who demands your silence or denies your right to grow."

– Alice Walker

Keyonna rushed to the door as the doorbell chimes rang through the house. She rose up onto her toes to look through the peep hole. With her friend in view, she started her happy dance and opened the door. "It's about damn time you came to my city!"

"Shut up," Venni said with a smile.

She walked in, and Keyonna set her luggage against the wall. "Welcome to Orlando, and to my shack."

"Shack, my ass," Venni replied as she looked up at the vaulted ceiling and admired the staircase with built-in bookshelves.

"Why did you get a cab? I thought Gabi was picking you up?"

"It wasn't that serious. I told her I'd just meet her over here."

Twelve-year-old Mya sprinted into the foyer with a cordless phone in her hand. She stopped to catch her breath and then gulped before she spoke. "Mom, can I go over Sydney's house?

She already asked her mom and she said it was okay. She said you can call her if you don't believe me."

"First of all...." Keyonna pointed to Venni.

Mya smiled sweetly. "Oh. Hi."

Venni waved.

"That's Miss Venni."

"Hi, Miss Venni."

"You must be Miss Mya. It's nice to finally meet you."

Mya's smile revealed the cutest little dimple in her left cheek.

Keyonna continued. "Now second of all, you need to go upstairs and get out of those sweaty clothes. You just got in from your game. What's the big rush? Take a shower, comb your hair, and then we'll talk about where you can go."

Mya dropped her shoulders and sighed softly. "Yes, ma'am." Her exit was much more subdued than her entrance as she moseyed down the hallway, barely lifting her feet.

"Whoa," Venni said. "Those eyes."

Keyonna raised her eyebrows and nodded. "Just like his. Right?"

"She's the perfect combination of you two. Beautiful."

Keyonna motioned for Venni to follow her into the kitchen. "Yeah. The trouble is I don't know if I want her to have either of our personalities."

Venni laughed. "You just don't want her to make some of the decisions y'all made."

"Yeah. That." Keyonna poured two glasses of wine. "Here. It's five o'clock somewhere."

"You sound like G," Venni said as she accepted the glass and smelled the drink. "So Mya plays ball? What position?"

"Point guard. And she's good."

"I love it. Where's Jasmine?"

"Taking a nap in the den. I needed her little hyper self to hit the pillow before she got in trouble. Mya wasn't rowdy like her when she was two. That girl is wearing me out. I blame Antonio."

Venni laughed.

Keyonna sipped but stopped prematurely. "Wait. Where's Lawrence?"

Venni raised her glass to her lips and took a long sip.

"That's okay. I'll wait."

"I'm no longer Lawrence's keeper. I don't know where he is."

"Say what? Y'all didn't break up, did you?"

"Yep. That ship has sunk. I gave him his money back for the plane ticket and told him not to come."

"Damn. Did he cheat or something?"

Before Venni answered, the doorbell rang again. Keyonna got up to answer it and came back with Gabriella.

"What the fuck, V? What happened to Lawrence?" she asked as soon as she entered the kitchen.

"Hey! I'm good. The flight was great. I'm excited to be in Orlando. How are you?"

Gabriella waved her hand. "Yeah, yeah, yeah. All of that. Why did you and Lawrence break up? Do I need my blade?"

Keyonna looked at Venni. "I filled her in already so you could pick up where we left off."

"No shit," Venni said.

"So...did he cheat?" Keyonna asked.

"No."

"Lie about something?"

"No."

"Mami…" Gabriella said sympathetically. "He isn't gay, is he? I knew he was being too patient about waiting for the cookie. He—"

"He's not gay!" Venni said with a frown. "I tried to tell him something important, and he left in the middle of the conversation. Not even in the middle."

Keyonna and Gabriella looked at her blankly, waiting for more. The sun beamed through the skylight, highlighting the pain Venni tried her best to mask. "And he never called again?" Keyonna asked.

"He calls all the time. Well, he used to. Either way, I'm done."

"What did Dr. Cox say?" Gabriella asked.

"About?"

"About Paris Hilton getting out of jail the other day," she replied sarcastically.

"I never told her about the breakup," Venni said.

Keyonna opened her mouth to ask 'Why?' but stopped before any sound came out. She glanced at Gabriella. They both knew not to push.

"Well, I have somebody else on my team tomorrow night!" Gabriella said.

"What team?" Keyonna asked.

"Team Single!" She chair-danced to the music in her head. Keyonna rolled her eyes, and Venni cracked a slight smile. "We'll be mingling while you're hugged up with the husby."

"Nah. I'm not mingling," Venni said.

"Too soon?" Keyonna asked.

Venni shook her head. "I'm done. Lawrence was that once-in-a-lifetime, accidental, slip-through-the-crack kinda guy. I'm okay with being alone. I'm complicated enough. I don't need someone else further complicating things."

"So if you saw him with another woman, you wouldn't care?" Gabriella asked.

"I already did."

"What?!" Gabriella and Keyonna said in unison.

"On TV. He was at a gala with the newscaster chick he was dating before we got together."

"How long have y'all been broken up?" Gabriella asked.

"Like a month and a half. We broke up at the end of April."

"You weren't pissed?" Keyonna asked. "My stiletto probably would've been through the TV screen."

"So I do need to cut him," Gabriella said.

Venni waved them off. "I can't be mad at him. I dismissed him. When I'm done, I'm done." Venni's words contradicted her tear-glazed eyes. She topped off her glass with more wine.

Keyonna poked her lip out. "But you were in love. It was all over your face, in your voice. This is sad. I'll be sad on your behalf."

"I'm not trippin'. Y'all are relationship-type girls. Look at you. You're married and giddy." She turned to Gabriella. "Once you slow your ass down, you'll be married with about ten babies."

Gabriella shook her head. "No thank you on the babies. And was that a shot at me because I'm Latina? Ten kids? Really?"

Keyonna laughed. Refilled her glass. "You're right, V. I've only had three boyfriends, and...." She looked over her shoulder and whispered. "Wait. Does Cole count?"

"Hell yeah, he counts!" Gabriella answered. "That crazy bastard."

"Okay. So, three boyfriends, and I married my last one."

Gabriella elbowed Venni. "She's about to get starry-eyed. Prepare."

Keyonna threw her napkin at Gabriella. It drifted onto the table before it reached her. "Whatever! Yes, I do love me some Antonio. And tomorrow when we're out, you're damned right. I won't mind being hugged up with my baby, thank you very much."

"Where is he anyway?" Venni asked. "I have to meet Mr. Wonderful in the flesh."

"Still at work," Keyonna said.

Mya ran into the kitchen and stood in the doorway. Her hair was brushed neatly into a ponytail, and her short denim shorts showed off her long legs. "Hi, Auntie G."

"Hey, mama. How was your game?"

"We won by twelve. I had thirteen points." She smiled proudly.

"Okay. I owe you thirteen dollars. I'll give it to you tomorrow." Gabriella winked.

"Thank you. Can I go now, Mom?"

"Be back by seven-thirty."

"Not eight?"

"Not a minute after. Bye!" Keyonna said. "Call me when you get there."

Mya jumped with joy and hurried away. "Yes! Thanks!"

Keyonna's birthday celebration was a classy affair. She'd rented out a private room in The Blue Note, a lounge downtown. Their party was a fairly small one, but once they ate dinner and mingled amongst themselves, the sixteen of them joined the hundreds of other patrons in the main area.

Blue fluorescent lights illuminated the place, creating a sexy vibe. The crowd was a mixture of twenty-one-year-olds who were trying out a different scene, thirty-year-olds who were there to show the youngins how it's really done, and forty-year-olds who were hoping to grind on twenty and thirty-year-old asses.

Venni had already been out on the floor for a while, courtesy of a chocolate cutie who said he played for the Tampa Bay Buccaneers. She rocked with him until his uninvited hands landed on her hips and slid back to her rear. When she swatted his hands, he blamed it on how sexy she looked in her leggings. Instantly, their club date was over. Without saying a word, she threw up the peace sign, holding her fingers just an inch away from his nose, and headed to the bar.

Gabriella was all about the single life and was used to ignorant happenings of that nature, but Venni wasn't built for it. Mr. Buccaneer reminded her why men disgusted her for years. Where was Camden when she needed him? Partying with her gay boy friends was much less invasive…and still tons of fun.

She sipped her drink and looked on as Antonio and Keyonna tore up the dance floor. They were clearly happy, and not just for the night. Such a cute couple. Their interaction reminded her of her and Lawrence's. Made her miss him. Made her order another drink.

She pulled out her phone and scrolled through her contacts. Selected Lawrence's name. Selected the text message icon. Started typing.

Gabriella danced her direction carrying two shot glasses. "Drink up, mama, so we can hit this floor!"

Saved by the belle. Venni exited the screen and downed the remainder of her mojito. She turned off her phone before accepting the glass from Gabriella. "Put this in your purse," she requested as she handed Gabriella her phone.

"You don't have room in yours?"

"Friends don't let friends drunk-text. Just do it, please." She held the shot glass to her lips and tilted her head back. Placed the empty glass on the bar.

Gabriella looked at her friend suspiciously and did as she was asked. She, too, downed her vodka and grabbed Venni by the hand. They sashayed in unison to an empty space on the dance floor. Soon, Keyonna and Antonio had joined them. After a wink from Keyonna, Antonio became the envy of the males who surrounded them when the ladies sandwiched him and rolled their bodies to the beat. R. Kelly's "I'm a Flirt" was already a great song, but the ladies made it unforgettable that night.

Keyonna was grateful to have spent her birthday with the closest people to her—especially Gabriella and Venni. The last time they were together for her special day, she'd turned seventeen and her world had been turned upside down. At twenty-nine, her world was right-side-up. The only thing that would make the night better was sure to happen once she and Antonio made it to their bedroom.

⊙≫⊙

Sunday had come much too quickly. Venni enjoyed the quick getaway with her girls in Orlando, but it was time to return to her big, empty house in Houston. She wouldn't be alone for long, though. Vance was coming in eight days and staying for three weeks.

Gabriella tapped her fingers on the steering wheel as they sat at a street light. She needed to say something. She glanced at Venni, who gazed out the window. She wondered what she was thinking. She wondered if her eyes showed her sadness behind the sexy sunglasses she was rocking.

"You thinking about Lawrence?" she blurted.

Venni jerked her head and looked at her friend. "What? Where did that come from?"

"I didn't want to talk about it too much at Keyonna's, but I...." She paused in an attempt to find the right words. "Fuck it. I'm just gonna say it. I think you're lying about how you really feel about the breakup, and I think you need to call him and make things right."

"You say that like I made things wrong!"

"He apologized, V. What else do you want from him? If he was still hounding you, you'd call him a little bitch. If there's something else you want, you need to tell him."

"I don't want anything from him."

"So why did you give me your phone last night? What were you gonna text him?"

Venni groaned. "I knew that's what this was about. Don't act like you haven't—"

"I'm not acting like anything. I drunk-text for sport. Sometimes, I pretend like I'm drunk, just because I can get away with saying whatever. You can't call me out."

"Just let it go."

"No. I don't like seeing my friends hurting. You know he's a good man. You've told him every single thing about yourself, and he still loves you. That shit isn't normal. You don't just throw that away."

"*Loved* me," Venni corrected. "He's moved on."

"With the anchor lady?" She pursed her lips. "Seat filler."

"Either way...."

"And for someone who says she doesn't care that she saw him with another chick, you're sure quick to bring that up."

"I only bring it up because it's the truth. And remember you started this conversation."

"You care, V. You can try to bullshit me, but stop bullshitting yourself."

"Why do *you* care?"

Once they reached the next light, Gabriella took her eyes off the road and glared at the woman she'd known since she was fifteen. "Don't do that."

Venni took in a deep breath and exhaled slowly. Gabriella had read her like a Dr. Seuss book—easily. There were many times she wanted to reach out to Lawrence, but she didn't know what she wanted to say. Now that she'd seen him with another woman attached to his arm, she was afraid he'd tell her to kick rocks. Barefoot. Lawrence really liked Cora Bradshaw, and if she hadn't run interference before he locked Miss Cora down, she was sure they would've been one of Houston's hottest couples.

"I'm not gonna call him and sound like the jealous ex."

"Who cares what you sound like? You want your man back!"

"But it'll look like I'm only reaching out because I saw them."

"Does he know you saw them? I thought you said it was on TV."

"Lawrence isn't stupid."

Gabriella pulled over and parked beneath the AirTran sign. "Neither are you. Stop acting like it. That foolish pride shit was excusable when we were twenty-one. We're too grown to not go after what we want. Keyonna has her happy ending. You're crazy close. You *putas* give me hope. We were two for three. Don't fuck it up."

Before Venni responded, Gabriella popped the trunk and got out of the car to get Venni's luggage. Venni met her at the rear of the car. "Did you call me stupid?"

"I said you're acting stupid. *Muy estupida.*" She gave her a quick hug. "Text me when you land."

Venni stood motionless, still shocked by Gabriella's words. Gabriella smacked Venni's butt with the back of her hand, got back into her car, and drove away. After Venni checked in and went through airport security, she pulled out her phone to check her email. There was a missed text message from Gabriella. Her first thought was that she'd left something in her car.

Last question. Did he ask for the ring back?

Venni had forgotten about the aqua box sitting on her dresser. It had become such a staple that she didn't think anything of it.

No.

Four minutes later, Gabriella texted back.

DON'T. BE. STUPID. Safe travels!

CHAPTER 15

Envy

*"But it is impossible to replace a person one
has loved with distractions."*

- Roald Dahl

Krave was arguably one of the top five strip clubs in the state of Texas. Venni's cousin, Aaron, introduced her to the place while they were in college. It quickly became one of her favorite hangouts. Unlike the nightclub scene, it provided music without the aggravation of men grinding on her or trying to take her home. At Krave, she could still hear the newest hits, eat some surprisingly tasty food, and enjoy the view while doing so. She'd admired her own womanly curves once puberty blessed her. Seeing other beautiful women showing off theirs gave her an odd sense of empowerment.

When Aaron invited her to join him for his birthday celebration, she was hesitant. Not only had she not been to Krave in over a year, her relationship with Aaron had been strained for three years. He reached out because he missed her. He wanted to repair their relationship, and he hoped revisiting their old stomping grounds would at least remind her of how much fun they used to have.

She agreed to come out, but only for a couple hours. It wasn't like she was doing anything else. She had reached out to Lawrence via text earlier that evening, but he never responded. Krave was the perfect distraction for her rejected spirit. She couldn't wait to get a few drinks in her so she could text Gabriella and cuss her out properly for making the suggestion in the first place.

They arrived at nine and sat at the side of the main stage. Popped bottles. Grooved to the music. Ate well. She'd just done this a week ago in Orlando, only the half-dressed girls making it clap in The Blue Note didn't get paid. They most likely didn't even get treated to breakfast at IHOP or Perkins once the place shut down.

Venni saw many familiar faces and a few new ones—college girls. There was one person missing, though. She hadn't seen her all night. "Does Envy still dance here?" she asked.

Aaron smiled like a child who was withholding a juicy secret. He shrugged, but it was clear that he knew. Venni reached for her purse.

"Alright then. I'm out," she said with a yawn. "This was nice. I missed your knucklehead."

"I thought you said you'd stay a couple hours," Aaron said, looking at his watch.

Venni shrugged and stood. An hour and a half was good enough.

"Y'all know what time it is," the deejay teased. "The main stage is about to be on fire. We gon' slow it down and let Miss Envy bless this thang. Think it's a game if you want to. They don't call her The Pole Goddess for nothin'. Already! Get them dollars out!"

Venni glanced at Aaron and took her seat again. He laughed and took a swig of his drink before giving Envy his full attention. The familiar sounds of Changing Faces' nineties hit blasted through the speakers. Men sat up straight in their seats in anticipation while most of the female patrons snapped their fingers and did an instinctive body roll. A soprano chorus of "Heyyyy!" filled the room.

The 5'7" vixen stood with her back to the crowd during the intro. Her tapping foot allowed for an immediate tease as her oiled-up muscles flexed under her cheeky leather shorts. When she turned around, those who had never seen her understood why her name was Envy. Her face was framed by curly hair that cascaded down to her D-cups. Her heavy mascara gave her a mystique that went well with her doe-like eyes. She licked her pouty lips as she surveyed her audience and let the song ask the question. Before she gave them what they'd come for, she smirked like an evil genius. She knew "Stroke You Up" would be a hit.

As she sashayed down the catwalk, she made eye contact with the ballers who held up wads of money, inviting her to earn it. Stopped in front of them to RSVP by unsnapping two of the three buttons on the right side of her shorts. Winked at the short one who tossed a handful of cash onto the stage.

Once she reached the pole, she got a little more comfortable. She rocked, rolled, and swirled to the groove, breaking free of the shorts and the crop top that had already given onlookers more than a peek at her "girls." It was showtime.

Envy showed her athleticism as she seductively climbed the pole and spun back down. When she gripped the pole and looked over her shoulder, she was surprised to see Venni, who smiled and shook her head. Instantly, the dance became an interpretive one—a visual dedication. Envy hadn't seen her in at least a year, and time had obviously been good to her. Venni was still sexy as ever with those green eyes.

Envy and Venni knew each other well—intimately, even. Their involvement was without definition. They weren't girlfriends, but everyone in Krave knew they were together. Strangers who saw them out and about knew they were together. And when they were together, their interaction was fiery. Envy was Venni's first girl crush, her first attempt at trying something new. They met when Venni was in a different place—when she was repulsed by men, bored with toys, and attracted to Envy's curves.

Their relationship wasn't just physical. They had a lot in common and would spend more time together at bookstores and in yoga sessions than in bed. They weren't out of touch because they had a falling out. Venni had fallen off. When Lawrence asked her to stay away from the strip club and expressed his discomfort with her remaining in contact with Envy, she respected his requests. He had been out on the town with the two of them. She'd shared stories with him. He'd even been in the other room a few times while Venni and Envy did their thing. So, he was well aware of their connection. Cutting ties with Envy didn't bother her a bit, but she couldn't deny that seeing those signature dance moves again affected her.

Venni cocked her head as Envy mounted the pole and flipped upside down. There was no doubt she was inviting Venni on a trip down Memory Lane. The question was did Venni mind accompanying her.

Aaron threw money onto the stage. "Damn! She still got it!" He elbowed Venni. "You see how she's lookin' at you?"

Venni crossed her legs and reached into her purse. She pulled out a one hundred dollar bill and held it between her two fingers. She normally wasn't that big of a tipper, but she didn't plan on visiting Krave again anytime soon. Though she held the bill casually, Envy spotted it. Subtly held up her finger and finished her show.

She was back out on the floor in fifteen minutes. She bypassed the men holding out money for lap dances and made her way over to Venni. Her smile was as bright as the stage lights.

Venni stood and held out the money. "What's up, Showtime?"

Envy accepted the tip with her teeth before tucking it into her garter. "What brings you here, Green? You must be single again."

"Be careful. You're fishing without a license," Venni replied.

Envy looked her up and down. "You look amazing."

"Trying to keep up with you," she flirted.

"Did you see Godiva?"

"Nah. She came back after having the baby? Where is she?" Envy pointed.

"Cool. I'ma go say hey to her and get outta here." She patted the seductress on her hip and nodded toward the thirsty onlookers. "Go make that money. It was good seeing you."

"Is your number still the same?" Envy asked.

"There's only one way to find out."

Venni gave Aaron a one-hand shoulder massage and winked at Envy in lieu of saying 'Goodbye.'

"Hey, Green," Envy called. When Venni returned her attention to her, she said, "Stay awake. Okay?" She turned and strutted away.

Venni smiled and turned away before the sway of Envy's hips hypnotized her. She found Godiva near the deejay booth and said a quick hello. Her visit to Krave had been fun, but it was time to go. The out-of-town crowd was starting to infiltrate the place, which usually guaranteed the occurrence of one major brawl. Besides, her stilettos were beginning to hurt her feet. Before she reached the door, she stopped and searched her purse for her valet ticket.

"Hey, V!" a voice called.

She looked up and saw one of the waitresses smiling and waving. She did the same. Also within view was a dark-skinned beauty who went by the name Jaguar. She was standing among a group of four guys; one of which was Lawrence.

Venni couldn't believe her eyes. Lawrence's disdain for the strip club was rooted in tragedy. His sister stripped for five years and was stalked by an obsessed patron who eventually followed her home one night after work. Lawrence was home from college at the time and was hanging out at her apartment. When he heard commotion outside, he ran out to see what was going on. He arrived just in time to take a bullet in his left shoulder for her. Unfortunately, the other two bullets missed him and hit their intended target. His sister died at age twenty-four. It had been thirteen years, but to hear him tell it, it felt like it happened yesterday.

But there he was smiling while Jaguar flirted with them. Venni greeted her with a subtle tickle to her ribs and leaned in to speak. Her lips brushed against Jaguar's ear. "Do your thing, mama." She tucked a fifty dollar bill in her cleavage and pointed to Lawrence.

Jaguar blew Venni a kiss and lowered herself onto Lawrence's lap. Venni could feel his eyes on her as she watched Jaguar pop, lock, and gyrate. She finally diverted her eyes toward his. Glared just long enough to acknowledge him. Strutted out the door.

"What the hell was that about?" Lawrence yelled to Venni who was halfway down the sidewalk.

She stopped mid-stride. "Who are you hollering at?" she asked as she handed her ticket to the valet.

"I thought you weren't into playing games," he said once he was within a few feet.

"And I thought you weren't into going to strip clubs."

Lawrence paused to regain his composure. The people nearby who were waiting in line to enter the club had become their audience, and he didn't want to make a scene. He lowered his volume and adjusted his tone to sound more civilized. "I'm here with Nick. I know you saw him. It's his birthday. I rode with him and Joe. They didn't tell me where we were going. Why were you there?"

"I was chillin'," Venni said casually.

"Yeah, okay. You saw Envy?"

"Of course I saw her. She was on the main stage."

"Did she see you?"

"Yup."

Lawrence laughed off his anger. "So you just gon' fuck with me?"

The driver pulled up with Venni's car and opened the door. "Listen. I'm about to go. Why don't you save all this concern for Cora's ass?"

"Cora? What's she got to do with this?"

"I saw the news, Lawrence. The gala? Yeah. That. Y'all were skinnin' and grinnin' like you'd skipped your way into your Disney happy ending."

"Venni, I took her to the gala because her date had the stomach flu. She called me that morning to see if I was available. Google her. She's dating the CEO of Dennison Oil. Or wait. I'll call her." He reached into his pocket, but was reminded that he was still waiting on his replacement phone. At work the day before, he'd dropped his Treo in the pool while he was helping an elderly lady get out safely.

"It's not that serious." She tipped the valet and stood at her door.

"You brought her up for the same reasons I brought up Envy. Real talk."

"Real talk, Cora Bradshaw ain't got shit on Envy. Go back inside. You'll see."

Lawrence stood with his arms folded and watched as Venni got into her car and drove away. He no longer had a claim on Venni, but the thought of her being with someone else still drove him crazy. If anyone had a chance of filling a vacancy for Venni, it was Envy. He couldn't dwell on it, though. Venni was moving on and he needed to do the same.

⚜

Venni lay in bed, mind spinning. She'd been trying to fall asleep since eleven, but it was 3 a.m. and she'd had a few cat naps at best. She was just dozing off again when her text message alert sounded. Only two people would feel comfortable texting her at that time of night. She checked to see which one it was. The name "Tiana"—Envy's government name—was next to the message icon.

```
Hey Green. I'm off. Wanna see u. It's raining
over here. Not money. Call me.
```

Venni tossed her phone onto the other side of the bed and rolled over. Had she received that text a year prior, she would've been dressed in ten minutes and at Envy's house within thirty. But with the tantalizing dance and memories of their chemistry aside, Envy was nothing but a good time. And that wasn't unique. Their lust wasn't unique. Anymore.

CHAPTER 16

Stuck

*"To fear love is to fear life, and those who fear
life are already three parts dead."*

– *Bertrand Russell*

There was an intensity in Venni's eyes when she walked into her living room away from home. Dr. Cox barely greeted her before she said, "I need to start this one off."

The doctor held out her hand, welcoming her conversation. "By all means."

Venni plopped onto the middle cushion of the couch and clasped her hands. "Remember when I said I was stuck between 'if' and 'when' after you asked where I am?"

Dr. Cox nodded.

"Remember I told you my mom has been talking to me in my dreams?"

"Of course."

"Well, there's no more debating. I have to tell Vance the truth. Soon."

"So there was another dream?"

"Yeah. Last night. For some reason, I was riding the train in Chicago. The car was packed. She got on and sat beside me but never said anything. I don't even know how there was room, because I was already sitting shoulder to shoulder with a Korean businessman and an old white lady. And I remember whispering to him that she smelled like cat pee." She shook her head in an effort to refocus. "Right before we got to my stop, my mom grabbed me by my shoulders and said, 'Dee, that boy needs to know you're his mother. Tell him the truth.'"

Dr. Cox listened intently.

Venni's focus remained on her expressive hands as she finished her story. "She only called me by my middle name when I was in trouble."

She described how violently her mother shook her. She recalled her mother saying something about "a year," but she couldn't put it into context. Dr. Cox could see the tiny beads of sweat forming on Venni's forehead as she pieced together the details of the dream.

"Still no clues on why it's so important to tell him now?"

"Not really. She said, 'The truth yields more truth,' and she kept saying, 'Secrets hurt.' Then she pulled off her wig." Venni closed her eyes briefly. "It was the one she wore the day she told me and Miles the truth about her cancer—the ugly one." She stopped. "Oh, my God. I just realized that."

"About the wig?"

Venni nodded. "She lied to us for months about her health. She thought she was protecting us by not telling us the truth, but by the time she told us it was cancer, she was dying. We didn't have time to wrap our minds around it before we lost her."

"So the gesture of pulling the wig off was to remind you of the pain you felt when she kept her diagnosis a secret."

"It had to be. And she had that same peach fuzz beneath it—the kind you could only see it if the light reflected off it a certain way. It was so real."

Venni sat with her thoughts. The click of the air conditioner interrupted the silence in the room, and its hum accompanied the present melancholy tone. The cool air swept in slowly, multiplying the goose bumps both women wore on their arms.

"There's a reason for this, Venni. And I'm afraid you won't know what it is until you initiate this conversation. It's been a long time coming. You and I know it's weighed on you. Vance is more than a sixteen-year-old secret. He's your son."

"I'm gonna tell him." Venni held her face between her hands and looked at the ceiling. "I just hope it's nothing crazy. I hope Tangie isn't sick and I don't know it. You know? That thing with my mom's wig is making me wonder. What if she's dying?"

"Well, prepare yourself for anything, but don't necessarily expect the worse. The bottom line is you'll never know until you tell her your intentions. He's coming to visit soon. Correct?"

"Tomorrow afternoon. I'm calling Tangie when I leave here."

"I support that decision. You and Vance deserve to love each other in truth," Dr. Cox said.

"I just have to make sure Tangie understands that I don't want to take him from her. I just want to clear the air."

Dr. Cox nodded. "And I'm sure she'll be quite resistant. This is a touchy issue. But remind her that you two dug this ditch together. If she's willing, invite her to be there when you tell him. It could give her a sense of security, knowing you want to include her in the conversation. And as far as Vance is concerned, it may take some of the sting away if you two are a united front. He won't feel like he has to choose a mother. He can possibly come to terms with having two women who love him the way only a mother can. He's too young to know the value in that, but when he gets older, he'll appreciate it."

Venni sighed loudly. "Teamwork makes the dream work. Right?"

Dr. Cox smiled softly. "You can do this. Have you given any more thought to telling Lawrence who Vance really is to you?"

"I told him in April, a few days after our session when I first told you about the dreams."

The doctor's eyes widened. "It's June and I'm just hearing of this?"

Venni shrugged. Dr. Cox thought for sure they'd made enough progress in her four months of therapy that she would've shared such big news. There had to be more to it.

"Well I'm proud of you for breaking your rule," Dr. Cox continued.

"It wasn't about breaking the rule. I just got tired of him sweatin' me about the dreams. He's a light sleeper. So, every time I was awakened from my sleep, so was he. He was pissed because I wouldn't tell him what was going on, so I just blurted it out one day."

"And?"

"It was too much for him to process, and he left. Now, he's hanging in strip clubs. So, whatever."

She explained further before she ran down a list of reasons—excuses—why she and Lawrence wouldn't have worked anyway. She was her usual fair and balanced self, careful not to place full blame on her ex. She chalked up their split as inevitable; saying nothing good in her life lasted.

"Since when did you become a victim, Ms. Miles?" Dr. Cox asked.

"I never said I was a victim."

"You're sure acting like one. The woman sitting in front of me today is a living, breathing cliché. You're certainly not the woman I met back in February."

"What's that supposed to mean?"

"You're not the woman for him. He needs a woman who doesn't have baggage. He deserves a woman who can appreciate his love. Shall I go on?"

"That's the truth. He's a great man. This isn't about him. It's—"

"—about you. Right?"

"Don't judge me."

"I have no gavel, no black robe, and my overage of sins disqualified me from getting a halo. I'm not here to judge you. I want you to see your actions for what they are. You're pushing Lawrence away because you're afraid."

Venni rolled her eyes. "Afraid of what?"

"Love."

Venni stared into space. "He said that."

"Smart man," Dr. Cox replied.

"I know love won't always be rainbows and candy hearts and Luther Vandross songs, but I don't want love if it makes me cry. If that's me being afraid, then…." She shrugged.

Now Dr. Cox understood why Venni cancelled appointments here and there and acted aloof when Lawrence's name came up in their sessions over the last month and a half. She was hurting from their breakup, and instead of talking about it, she held it in. She was trying to avoid the conversation they were now having.

Dr. Cox slid toward the edge of her chair and removed her glasses. "Venni, I'm about to say something that's probably gonna piss you off." Venni raised an eyebrow as the doctor continued. "You should thank Lawrence for making you cry. I actually celebrate him for making you cry."

"So it's cool that he hurt me."

Dr. Cox held up her pen. "Stop. Lawrence made you feel. You *let* yourself feel, and that was our goal. Crying is an expression of numerous emotions. You're not just hurt. Some of those tears come from frustration, from missing him, from remembering all the other times he didn't make you cry. You were okay with the rainbows and candy hearts and Luther songs. When the clouds and sour grapes came into play, you ran. Suddenly you were emotionally unavailable again. That's not fair to Lawrence. It's not fair to you. And you know it."

"That's why I removed myself! I'm not cut out for love. That's why I broke up with him," Venni shot back.

"Have you cried since the breakup?"

Venni smirked and shook her head but remained silent. The doctor sat back in her chair. Crossed her legs. Waited.

Finally, Venni spoke. "Are we just gonna sit here now?"

"I'm waiting for an answer."

"I just told you—" She stopped herself. "Oh, so you want me to say it. You win. Okay? I get your point."

"I'm not your opponent. We're on the same team, Venni."

"Yes, I've cried since the breakup. Quitting him didn't stop the tears." Venni wasn't sure what was worse: the act of crying or talking about crying.

"So now what?" Dr. Cox asked.

"That's my line."

"I'm only here to give you perspective. I can't make decisions for you. I'll tell you this, though: contemplation without action is why you're stuck between 'if' and 'when.'"

Venni looked away and shook her head. Coached herself into not cussing out the doctor as she counted the ticks she heard from the nearby clock.

The tension in the room began to smother Dr. Cox. She tapped out after seventeen ticks.

"There's plenty more to be explored, Venni. I'm not here to alienate you." Her tone was softer. "You asked me to go on this journey with you. I won't avoid navigating through the murky issues and letting you trip over the truth. But I won't leave you, either…unless you ask me to."

Venni never changed her posturing.

Dr. Cox stood and walked to her desk. "We'll continue this next time. Today, let your takeaway be this: You know what you need to do. When it feels right, do it. That applies to Vance *and* Lawrence."

CHAPTER 17

No More Lies

"There are only two mistakes one can make along the road to truth; not going all the way, and not starting."

– Buddha

Vance stood at his bed and arranged his sneakers neatly in his duffle bag. His suitcase lie next to it with a mound of clothes piled inside. Tangela leaned against the doorframe and watched her son prepare for his trip the next day.

He was always so excited to go visit Venni. As usual, he'd asked about his flight information at least ten times that week. He'd washed all of his clothes the previous weekend and packed the majority of them. Any other time, Tangela had to threaten his life for him to even step inside the laundry room. He couldn't wait until morning, and his body language proved that. He maneuvered around his room with his headphones on, bobbing his head to the beat of the music and rapping along.

Tangela lived to make him happy, but accepting his love for Venni didn't get easier as the years went by. He loved her immensely and automatically, and he didn't even know why.

But Tangela did. Though she was his mother in every way that mattered, Venni often got the glory; not for raising him, but for being so "cool" and giving the best gifts. A piece of Tangela's heart broke every year he went to her sister's house for his summer visit.

She knocked on his door to get his attention. After a second, louder knock, Vance turned around. "Everybody's here. We're about to sing and cut the cake."

Vance set his headphones on the bed. "Okay." He started toward the door.

"Put on a t-shirt."

Vance did as he was told, slipping a t-shirt over the wife-beater he was wearing. Tangela smiled with pride as she watched her little man who now looked more like a grown man descend the steps in front of her. This was not a time for sad faces. In spite of the circumstances, she was blessed with two children, and one was celebrating her first year of life.

Twenty-three guests surrounded the dining room table and sang "Happy Birthday" to Kayla, who grinned and grabbed a hunk of her personal cake before the song was over. Theodore nearly had a conniption, while everyone else laughed hysterically. Tangela played photographer, trying her best to capture every moment. Her favorite: the priceless shot of Vance holding his little sister and helping her blow out the candle on the larger, undestroyed cake.

She wanted to have the party while Vance was still in town, and that meant celebrating Kayla's birthday on the actual day—a Tuesday. Even though it was a weekday, everyone who mattered showed up. Tangela's mother drove in from Chicago with Tangela's aunts and uncle. Theodore's parents flew in from

Pennsylvania. The remainder of the guests were coworkers and friends the couple had met during their time in the D-M-V area. She was grateful to all of them for helping to make her miracle baby's day special.

The phone rang at about eight o'clock. It was Venni. She stayed in her bedroom to take the call, but alerted Theodore to stay downstairs with Kayla until she was done talking. Venni didn't waste too much time before she got to the point of her call.

"Listen. I've been having some crazy dreams since March. I'll spare you the details, but basically, my mom is telling me that it's time to tell Vance the truth."

"What truth?" Tangela asked suspiciously.

"Well, he's known for years that the Easter Bunny, Tooth Fairy, and Santa weren't real. So…."

"You can't be serious."

"Let me first say that I don't want anything to change. I'm not telling him in hopes that he'll want to abandon you and come live with me."

"That would never happen anyway." Tangela's tone reeked of cockiness. "And I haven't agreed to you telling him a damn thing."

Venni bit her tongue. Literally. She reminded herself that Tangela's reaction was natural. Tangela loved Vance as if he was hers, and she perceived Venni as a potential threat to their relationship. Venni needed to choose her words carefully or risk Tangela not putting Vance on the plane the next day.

"Tangie, breathe. I'm just tired of secrets and lies. This one is the only one weighing me down now, and it took my mom calling me out on it to provoke some action. Vance is old enough. He's sixteen, very mature for his age. I think he can handle it. It's all in how we present it."

"You can't exactly wrap this up with fancy paper and put a pretty bow on it, Venni. Thinking he can handle this type of news shows how out of touch you are. I'm his mother. I know better."

More tongue-biting. "This isn't a competition, Tangie. And really, I'm not asking for your permission. I'm letting you know that before Vance leaves Houston to come back home, he will know what you and I did sixteen years ago. I would like us to tell him together. That's what I was going to propose before you reminded me that you're his mother."

"And you think that's gonna make a difference?"

"It'll make a world of difference. It's gonna be awkward and confusing no matter what, but if we tell him together, he won't feel like we're asking him to choose a mother. Not only that, you could explain your motives behind the adoption without me paraphrasing for you."

"I can't believe you. No one will benefit from this. Somehow you've convinced yourself that you will, but you won't," Tangela said.

"We're all entitled to our opinions. Ultimately, everyone benefits. If something ever happens to Vance and he needs blood…."

"You never struck me as the *Lifetime*–movie-watching type."

Venni laughed her off.

"So have you picked a date for your big reveal?" Tangela asked.

"I was thinking we could tell him after the London trip. He's scheduled to fly home a few days after that. You could come here and fly back with him."

"You've got it all figured out, huh?"

"Actually, I don't," Venni replied. "But—"

"Well, I'm gonna hang up now. Thank you for ruining my otherwise fabulous day."

"You know that wasn't my intent. It's never bothered you that we've been lying to him all this time?"

Click.

Venni checked her cell phone signal. Four bars. "Call Ended" flashed on her screen. She almost called back, but she decided to let Tangela be. She planned to touch base with her the next day. Maybe she would be a little more level-headed. Or not. Either way, Venni had stated her intentions. It was up to Tangela to decide whether she wanted to be a team player.

Tangela flung the cordless phone across the room. It hit the wall, ricocheted off the night stand, and landed on the floor in pieces. "Selfish bitch! Where the hell did this come from?" she screeched as she walked aimlessly around the space.

"Ma, you okay?" Vance yelled from his room.

"I'm fine. The phone fell," Tangela yelled back.

She plopped onto the bed and mumbled a medley of expletives. Theodore rushed in a few minutes later with Kayla in his arms. Her head was nestled near his neck and her eyes were closed. "Did something happen?" he asked.

Tangela's bloodshot eyes spoke for her when she glanced at her husband.

"Let me lay her down," Theodore said.

When he returned, he began gathering the scattered pieces of the phone. "What did C-O-HO do?"

"Stop. You're not gonna disrespect her like that. She's still my sister. She's got issues, but she's still my sister," Tangela said before telling him about her conversation with Venni.

Theodore sat on the bed and rested his head in his hands. "So she's saying her dead mother has convinced her to tell Vance?" he asked with deadpan expression.

"Is that the most ridiculous shit you've ever heard or what?"

He shook his head. "I knew this would happen."

"Now is not the time for 'I told you so,'" Tangela snapped.

"I didn't say that, Tangela. But I knew she would do this at some point. I thought she would've done it sooner, though." After some contemplation, he spoke again. "Basketball."

"What?"

"Things are picking up. More schools are calling. As much as I hate it, we all know he'll be going to a major university on a basketball scholarship. She wants the glory. She wants to say that's her son. How many times have we heard her tell the story of buying his first basketball?"

Tangela wanted to agree with him, but her heart knew better. Venni was an opportunist, but only when it came to business matters. If Vance was destined to be a cab driver or a custodian, she would love him the same.

"And we both know how much she loves money. That dates back to her days at Exquisite. If Vance is as good as these coaches make him out to be, he'll be a millionaire at age twenty-two," Theodore continued. "What you need to do is call her out. Tell her if she wants to tell the truth, she needs to tell the whole truth. I bet she doesn't want him to know she was getting paid to screw his father and anyone else whose bank account was fat enough. She was making them feel special, when it was really all a lie. She's doing the same thing to Vance, just in a different capacity. She's selfish."

Tangela paused for a moment to let his words register. She had shared some details about Venni's prostitution stint, but she didn't remember telling him the name of the hotel she worked in. Theodore was no dummy, though. Since Venni also had a legitimate job there working the front desk, he had most likely put two and two together. His animosity, though, was quite alarming.

"V's not like that. Money is not her motivation for doing this. That, I'm sure of. Between her mom's insurance policy, our dad's policy, her money from Lakeside, and her salary, she's set."

"So if her request is so harmless, why are you upset?"

"Because this came out of left field. We never said we would tell him the truth—not even once he was an adult. I fully committed to being his mother, and she fully committed to being his aunt. Period. Now, she wants to explain this to him? How do we explain this to him?"

"Exactly. So, help me understand. After she tells him this, what does she want to happen?"

"Nothing. She's not trying to lure him away from us. She just wants him to know the truth so there won't be any secrets between them. You know she's been in therapy trying to free herself and cleanse her soul—all that rah rah. I guess this is part of her healing." She rolled her eyes.

They sat in silence for a few moments. "Don't put him on the plane," Theodore said.

"That won't solve anything. If anything, it'll create more problems. He'll be livid if he can't go to Houston. Besides, Venni can tell him over the phone if she wants."

"So, you're admitting that you have no control."

Tangela's voice rose an octave. "You know how close they are. You saw that when we started dating; when he was two."

"You never should've let them become so close." He shook his head. "I don't understand how you don't want to raise your child but insist on seeing him every year."

Tangela sighed. "You know why she gave him to me. Don't make this into something it isn't."

"And there you go defending her again. You need to decide what your stance is when it comes to dealing with that woman. On one hand, you cry about how you're the one who has raised him and you hate that she feels a sense of entitlement to be in his life. On the other hand, you facilitate their relationship and defend her past as a whore. I don't get it."

"I defend her in general because she's my sister."

"*Half*-sister. And your dad disowned her for a reason. I don't respect her, and quite frankly, I'm starting to not respect you."

Tangela waved her hands dismissively. "This conversation is over. I thought you wanted to talk, but it seems you'd rather wage war. I'm not equipped for this shit tonight, Theodore."

Theodore stood and strolled to the master bathroom, disrobing along the way. "Go ahead. You two sit down and tell that boy that his whole life has essentially been a practical joke. I wish you the best. While you're at it, why don't you tell her about Kayla, too?"

He continued to spew sarcastic comments from inside the bathroom. Tangela was glad when he finally turned on the water and got into the shower. Though he was probably still barking his I-told-you-so's, she couldn't hear a thing. To ensure she wouldn't have to listen to him once he finished, she changed into her pajamas and went into Kayla's room. She stood at the crib and watched her sleeping beauty for a few minutes. Temporarily forgot about her worries.

She pulled back the sheets on the twin bed across the room and settled in.

Joy will come in the morning, she thought. *It has to.*

The morning came, but Tangela's joy didn't. She put on a happy face anyway and drove Vance to the airport. They stood at the security checkpoint among the herd of passengers and read the flight information on the monitors.

"Well, it looks like it's departing on-time," she said as Vance untied his sneakers and took them off. "Why are you doing that already?"

"It just makes it easier when I get up there, Ma. I got this," he replied.

"Excuse me," she said with a smirk.

His text alert sounded and he checked the message. Texted back.

"Who is that?"

"Aunt V."

"What did she say?"

"She was just asking if I was at the airport yet," Vance replied with a hint of irritability.

"Alright. I guess you should get going." She motioned for him to come closer and gave him a hug. She held him tightly as tears rolled down her cheeks.

When they separated, Vance noticed she was more emotional than usual. She always cried when he went away—even if it was for a weekend basketball camp; but this time, she was on the brink of bawling.

"You okay?" he asked.

She nodded and wiped her face. Straightened his shirt. "Remember, don't—"

"I know," Vance interrupted. "Don't mention Kayla." He leaned down and kissed his little sister, who was asleep in her stroller.

Tangela's phone rang loudly in her purse.

"Love you, Ma. I'll call you when I get there," Vance said over his shoulder as he rushed away.

Tangela knew who was calling before she looked at the screen. "Yes," she answered.

Venni expected the less-than-pleasant greeting. "Tangie, you don't have to be like—"

"He's going through security check right now, Venni. I'm not holding him hostage. Okay?"

"I really believe it's gonna be okay," Venni reassured.

"I'm afraid I don't agree. Maybe you should send me whatever Kool-Aid your therapist has you drinking."

"I'll tell you what. Call me when you're ready to set the sarcasm aside and speak like an adult."

"There's nothing more to say. Just stick to your end of the deal. Don't say anything until I get there. I'll let you know what day I'm coming next month."

CHAPTER 18

Mr. Too Damn Good

"Love is never lost. If not reciprocated, it will flow back and soften and purify the heart."

– Washington Irving

Venni and Vance didn't make it past the kitchen after their busy afternoon. They sat at the table and chatted about her work schedule, his play schedule, and the boys down the street she wanted to introduce him to. As usual, he was looking forward to his three weeks in Houston. His aunt never let him down. She always had a concert, party, or weekend getaway planned for them. Most summers, they partook in all three. This year, he was set to accompany Venni on a business trip overseas.

"Where's L?" Vance asked once there was a lull in their conversation.

Venni was shocked it took him that long to ask about Lawrence. She expected the question during the ride home from the airport, but apparently their stop at his favorite Mexican restaurant for a late lunch and impromptu shopping trip at The Galleria bought her some time. And once they made it home and she nonchalantly opened the garage door to reveal his birthday surprise, Vance wasn't thinking of anything unrelated to sitting behind the wheel of that Chrysler. Now, it was nightfall, and she was all out of distractions.

"Probably at his house," she answered.

"Call him and tell him to come over. He knows I'm here. Right?"

Venni twisted her lips.

Vance tapped his phone screen. "Never mind. I can hit him up myself." The phone rang loudly on speaker.

"Hang up, Vance."

"Why?" Just as he went to tap the End button, Lawrence picked up.

"Big V!" Lawrence's surprise was evident. Venni could feel him smiling through his words.

"Yo!!!" Vance replied. "When are you comin' over, man? I'm ready to whoop you in Live."

Lawrence and Vance were fierce but friendly competitors in the Xbox game, often acting as if they were actually NBA stars competing for the title. Vance loved him some Lawrence from the time he first met him. He was thirteen, and Lawrence invited Venni to bring him to his house for a pool party. After a series of races in the pool, a lesson on barbequing, and a game of H-O-R-S-E, Vance had found a new buddy to hang with during his visits to Houston.

"Um…what did your aunt say about that?" Lawrence asked.

Vance glanced at Venni. "She didn't say nothin'."

"Why don't you ask her if you can come over here and—"

Venni spoke up. "Lawrence, you're on speaker. I don't care if you come play the game."

Lawrence paused. "Okay. Cool. I'll come over tomorrow at about three."

"Aw, I get it. You probably have to practice all night before you go against the champ. That's what's up," Vance replied.

"Nah, little buddy. I just don't want your first night in town to be the worst night of your vacation. I'll show you tomorrow, though. You know talk is cheap."

"Yeah yeah. Alright, man," Vance said with a wide grin. His joy was contagious. Venni couldn't help but smile, too. "Oh! You have to see my whip, too. Or wait. You already saw it, huh?"

Lawrence chuckled. "Yeah, I saw it, but I gotta see how you look in it; make sure you got the lean right."

"Aunt V said I can drive to the courts this weekend. You gotta teach me how to wax this thing so I can be on-point."

"I got you." After Lawrence finished snickering, there was a moment of hesitation. "Alright, V. Miles. I'll see y'all tomorrow."

"Yep," she said softly.

"Boooooo! That was weak!" Vance said. "Y'all don't have to front because y'all on speaker phone. Go 'head." He mimicked the two of them saying, "I love you. No, I love you. But I love you more."

Venni rolled her eyes and reached for Vance's phone so she could hang up. Before she touched the screen, Lawrence said, "She knows how I feel."

She paused. Tapped the End button. Turned to Vance, who was still laughing.

"Heart-to-heart time," she said. "Lawrence and I aren't together anymore."

Record scratch. "What? Why not?"

She shrugged. "Just the way it goes sometimes, kiddo."

Vance sat forward in his chair. "I'm sorry."

"For what? You didn't know," Venni answered.

"For inviting him over. I can tell him never mind if you want."

"Vance, it's fine. He can come over. He's your friend. That shouldn't change because he and I broke up."

Vance was bummed. Venni's demeanor was so different when Lawrence became more than her friend. She was never a Debbie downer, but she smiled more and laughed harder. Her eyes lit up when she talked about him. In her own, cool way, she acted like the people on TV when they were in love.

"Do you think you guys will get back together?"

Venni played with a piece of paper on the table. "You really like him, huh?"

"He's a cool dude. Hold up. He didn't cheat on you. Did he?"

Venni chuckled. He sounded like Keyonna. "No."

"Okay. Yeah. He's a cool dude. I never saw you with anyone else, and when you were with him, you always seemed happy."

"Contrary to popular belief, babe, 'always' has an expiration date."

"What if you put it in the freezer?" Vance raised an eyebrow and wagged his index finger.

She loved engaging in battles of wit with him. He was quick and bold. He was clever. He was undeniably her child.

Later that night, she stood at her dresser and took out her earrings. She set them next to her perfume, which was next to the ring box that had become a part of her bedroom decor. She stared at the box. Picked it up. Opened it.

"*She knows how I feel.*" Lawrence's words echoed in her head. She removed the black velvet box from within and flipped up its top. The emerald cut solitaire was two carats of flawlessness. It was perfect for her. Simple, yet stunning.

She hadn't looked at it since last July when Lawrence gave it to her. Eleven and a half months later, there it was in her hand, still sparkling, even though her relationship with Lawrence had dulled. She couldn't lie to herself. She missed him. And Vance rooting for him only intensified her thoughts of humbling herself and reaching out to the man she once called her lover and friend.

Venni returned the box to its original spot and squatted at the foot of her bed, next to her purse. She found what she was looking for in just a few seconds. It was the CD Lawrence asked her to listen to back in May—the CD that had remained in her car untouched until nosey Vance discovered it in her glove compartment on their way home from the airport. Really, she had forgotten about it until he pulled it out and asked what was on it. She lied and told him it was blank, knowing she could still have been emotionally unprepared for what Lawrence wanted her to hear. While Vance unloaded his luggage from her car, she slipped the disc into her purse.

Her initial intent was to put the CD in her armoire and listen to it at her convenience. As she unzipped her purse, it was obvious her intentions had changed. She put the disc into her player and lay diagonally on her bed. When she pressed Play on the remote, the intro to the first song immediately sounded familiar. When she heard the first few ad libs, she knew what she was listening to. It was Babyface, and he was asking "Where Will You Go?"

She stared at the wall ahead as she listened to the lyrics that hit home. What made her split with Lawrence most hurtful was that she hadn't just lost her boyfriend; she'd lost her best friend. He was the only person in Houston she'd truly embraced. He knew her secrets, her details; why she didn't drink milk or like dogs. He knew what made her laugh, but he never knew what made her cry. Now he did. He wasn't supposed to be the one to reopen her tear ducts. He was supposed to be her "good guy"—a term they'd used jokingly from the time he first asked her out.

Venni felt like a sappy fool. Though she didn't burst into a thousand tears, the few that seeped out were indicative of the residual and unresolved feelings she had for the man Gabriella and Keyonna said was almost too good to be true. Let Dr. Cox tell it, her tears were proof that she was finally allowing herself to feel. She closed her eyes as the next song began. Gerald Levert crooned "Mr. Too Damn Good," the perfect description of Lawrence.

The two songs looped over and over on repeat until seven-thirty the next morning. They tortured her mind and soothed her spirit at the same time. She accepted the truth in the lyrics. She accepted that she needed to make things right with the man she loved.

⌾∞⌾

"Don't come up in here with that!"

"That was a foul all day!"

Venni could hear Lawrence and Vance trash-talking from the bottom of the stairwell. Over the past three summers, she'd grown accustomed to hearing them make bets and argue about who was the best at playing the video game. Their voices made the place sound like home.

She ascended the steps and peeked into Vance's room. "Just letting you know I'm here."

"What's up, Aunt V?" Vance said, never looking away from the screen.

Lawrence turned and gave Venni his full attention. His eyes softened as soon as they connected with hers. "Hey."

"Hey."

"Caught you slippin'!" Vance taunted after his player dunked on Lawrence's.

"I won't interrupt your game. I'm ordering pizza in a little bit if y'all want some."

"Pepperoni and mushrooms," Vance said.

Venni looked at Lawrence, waiting for an answer. He bucked his eyes, shocked that he was included in the offer. "The usual?" she asked.

"Yeah. That's cool. Thanks," he replied.

"Alright. You better get back to that game before he has you streaking through the neighborhood or detailing his car with a toothbrush." She smiled and continued to her room.

The next Friday, Lawrence was at the house again. Vance had texted Venni at work so she knew to expect company when she got home. Early in the week, she'd made plans to go to Fire Lounge with Camden and his new boo-thang, so she figured she wouldn't be home until he was long gone.

When she did arrive, she was surprised to see Lawrence's car still parked in her driveway. She wasn't prepared to see him again. She wasn't unhappy about seeing him, either. Being around him triggered emotions that she had trouble fighting, though.

"*You know what you need to do. When it feels right, do it.*"

"*We're too grown to not go after what we want.*"

Dr. Cox and Gabriella's words replayed in her mind as she stepped out of her heels and headed upstairs. Instead of stopping at Vance's room, she went to her own. Took a shower. Thought some more. Once she slipped into her more comfortable attire, she knocked on Vance's open door.

"Aunt V! When did you get here?" Vance asked after a quick glance.

"About a half hour ago. Somebody could've robbed the place. Y'all didn't even see me walk by."

Vance laughed. "My bad."

Lawrence didn't answer because he was too busy admiring the long, oiled up legs next to him. Venni was wearing his favorite shorts—the black cotton ones that were just barely long enough to wear around Vance.

Venni placed her hand on his shoulder. "I need to talk to you for a minute, please."

He barely had time to acknowledge her request before she disappeared from the doorway. He looked at Vance, who wore the same curious expression on his face. Vance shrugged.

"Let's shut it down for the night, man. It's late, and I think I've officially worn out my welcome," Lawrence said before he stood and reached his arms toward the ceiling. "We may have to start hanging out outside of the house. I'll call you next week sometime. We can hit up the go-cart spot."

"Bet."

Lawrence stepped out of the room and looked left and right. Venni's room light was on, and her door was cracked. He approached with caution and peeked inside. Knocked twice.

"Come on," Venni said.

When Lawrence entered, she was seated at the foot of her bed with her hands clasped between her knees. "You okay?" he asked.

She spoke calmly and softly. "Answer my question first. Why didn't you text me back the night I saw you at Krave?"

Venni was good for coming out of left field with information or questions, so Lawrence wasn't too taken aback by her query. "I didn't get a text from you."

"Well, I *sent* you a text a couple hours before I went."

"Oh!" Lawrence said after he thought a little longer. "I didn't have a phone. It had fallen in the pool at work." He pulled his phone from his pocket. "See? I had to get a replacement."

Venni could see that the phone was new. The screen was cracked on his other one. She felt a sense of relief. Lawrence wasn't ignoring her that night.

"Is that why you went to Krave? Because I didn't text back?" he asked.

"Aaron asked me to go. And to get back to your question, no, I'm not okay." Lawrence sat next to her. Venni's nerve endings danced once his thigh touched hers. The scent of his body wash was aromatherapy. "I've been acting like I'm okay, but I'm not," she added.

"What happened?" he asked.

Venni exhaled slowly before she spoke. "My heart picked a fight with my pride, and my heart won."

"So what's that mean? Are you ready to talk now?"

"It means I miss you."

Lawrence couldn't believe his ears.

"I owe you a real apology," Venni continued.

"I know you—"

"I finally listened to the CD last week."

"What did you think?"

"I cried."

Lawrence's eyes widened. "I wasn't trying to make you cry."

Venni offered a slight but reassuring smile. "It's okay."

"Those songs…that's how I feel."

"Feel or felt?" she asked.

"You heard me."

Venni cut her eyes at him. "And I Googled Cora's boyfriend."

He smiled, knowing that was Venni's way of admitting she cared. Though he'd been longing for Venni to reach out to him, he certainly didn't expect her to. Her honesty was always one of her sexiest traits, and there she was bringing sexy back.

She rested her hand on his thigh. "I took your patience for granted, and I'm sorry for that. I shut down instead of talking because I thought it would be easier. I'm not proud of all the changes I put you through. You're a good—no, great—man. Superman."

He peeked inside his t-shirt.

Venni laughed. "What are you doing?"

"I was checking for my 'S.'"

Venni was willing to pull his shirt off and show him the 'S' on his chest, but she kept her thoughts and her hands to herself.

"All kidding aside, though, you just made my week. Apology accepted." He placed his hand on top of hers. Paused and lifted it slowly. When he looked down, the engagement ring he'd given her almost a year to the date prior sparkled atop Venni's finger. His brow never had so many wrinkles. He looked up at her. "What's up with this?"

Venni took in another deep breath. "I've had a lot of time to think while we've been apart. I searched my soul, searched my heart. All I kept finding was you. Apparently this love stuff doesn't wear off after a couple months." She toyed with the ring. "I figured since the feeling won't go away, why would I want you to? If you let me, I wanna show you why you should come back into my life and why you should stay. Forever."

Lawrence stared at the ring for a while. "How do I know you won't walk away again?"

"You don't. You won't know until the time comes for me to show and prove."

"So you're asking me to take a leap of faith?"

"I'm asking you to let me love you the way you've loved me all along. I thought you left the ring here for a reason. If the offer's off the table, I understand." She slid the ring off and offered it to Lawrence.

To her surprise, he took it. "You know, leaps of faith with you are more like intense plyometric workouts," Lawrence said as he stood. He kept his eyes on the ring. "Did you hook up with Envy?"

"I could've, but no."

"You haven't seen her since that night at Krave?"

Venni shook her head. "I don't need a cheap thrill."

Lawrence nodded and knelt in front of Venni. Grabbed her left hand. "Good, because I did leave this here for a reason." He slid the ring onto Venni's finger and kissed her hand. "I guess this means we're back together, V. Miles."

CHAPTER 19

Caught Up

"There are no secrets time does not reveal."

— Jean Racine

Venni was awakened from her sleep when she tried to straighten her legs and was stopped abruptly. When she blinked the blurriness away, she saw that her big toe was stuck in one of the openings of a laundry basket that was jammed against the wall.

"What the hell?" she grumbled as she freed her toe.

Her head was pounding, and the smell of clean linen dryer sheets wasn't helping any. Lawrence lay across from her, still fast asleep, with her gray silk robe draped over his lower body. She sat up and looked over her shoulder to find that she was using a pile of clean towels in lieu of a pillow. Reached to her right to confirm what she was already sure of. Touched the dryer. Yep. They were in the laundry room.

She shook Lawrence until he woke up. He was just as disoriented as she. "Where are my clothes?" he asked once he peeked under the robe.

She shrugged. "I don't know, but you see what happened to my panties." She pointed to the lacy thong that was draped around her left ankle, ripped.

There was extended silence and then hysterical laughter from both of them.

"I knew we shouldn't have messed with that tequila. Jose gets me in trouble every time," Lawrence said.

"Shit, apparently me, too. How did we end up in here?" Venni asked. "Weren't we in the bedroom?"

"At first. You don't remember us coming down here to take shots?" He stood up.

Venni pointed. "You have a dryer sheet stuck to your booty, baby."

Lawrence swatted it off and picked up the empty tequila bottle. "I gotta find my clothes."

Venni gasped. "Do you think they're in the kitchen? I do remember what happened on the counter." She smiled and shuddered. When she returned to present-day, she was in near-panic mode again. "What if Vance has been down here? What time is it?"

"Baby, do you see a watch on me?"

She opened the dryer and searched for something to throw on. She found a tank top and some sweats. "Why am I sticky?" she asked as she got dressed. She took the empty liquor bottle from Lawrence and instructed him to stay there while she checked the kitchen for their clothes.

She crept out of the room and into the hallway like a teenager who had returned home after sneaking out. The coast was clear. Vance wasn't downstairs. She scurried to the kitchen, nearly tripping over a can of whipped cream on her way. That explained why she was sticky. There were no clothes in sight, though.

She even went into the living room and searched the couch cushions. Nothing. Before she returned to the laundry room, she went back to the kitchen and sprayed disinfectant on the counter she and Lawrence had occupied. She figured it needed to set for a while before she wiped it off anyway.

Lawrence was understandably annoyed to hear that his clothes weren't down there. It wasn't like he could put on any of Venni's clothes that were in the dryer. "Just bring me some shorts from your room. I know I have a few pairs here."

Venni folded her lips.

"Did you burn 'em or something?" he asked.

She shook her head. "I packed all your things in boxes so I wouldn't have to look at 'em."

"Do you know where they are? Garage?"

"In my storage unit."

"Across town?"

"Babe…" Venni said slowly and apologetically. "I hated you. I didn't want the stuff in my vicinity and you said you didn't want it back. I had to get it out of here. We'll go get the boxes today."

"That doesn't help me right now."

"Shh…." She held her held. "I didn't take Tylenol yet. Just wrap up in one of those towels and go to the room. "V won't think twice if he sees you like that."

Before Lawrence left the room, Venni pinched his butt. "Wait for me before you get in the shower. I'ma wipe down the counter and take some medicine."

Venni scurried down the hall in anticipation of joining her man in the shower. She missed those intimate moments during their time apart. Just as she passed Vance's room, she heard his door open.

"Aunt V," he called.

She backpedaled and walked inside. "What's up, babe?"

"Can I talk to you real quick?"

Vance sat in bed with his head resting on the wall. His eyes looked watery and distressed. Venni had never seen him like this, and she immediately worried that Tangela jumped the gun and told Vance that he wasn't her son.

"Yeah. You okay?" she asked as she sat at the foot of his bed. She nudged his ankle.

"I don't wanna upset you, but I have to talk to somebody."

Now Venni was really confused. What could he say that would upset her? "I'm your somebody. Talk to me."

"Ava missed her period."

Venni's eyes bucked under her raised eyebrows. She knew Vance traded v-cards with Ava for his birthday and was excited that he'd experienced what his teammates and friends were always bragging about. Apparently, though, he'd forgotten to enjoy his new experiences with condoms.

Venni took a deep breath before she spoke. "How late is she?"

"Two weeks." Vance's voice cracked. "I know," he said as Venni buried her face in her hands.

"We talked about protection in February. What's the deal? Were you just being reckless?"

"She said she was on the pill."

"And if I recall correctly, I told you not to trust any female who says that. Did you give her a pill every day and watch her swallow it?" She held up her hand. "It's rhetorical."

Vance hit his head against the wall a few times.

"Giving yourself a headache isn't gonna help. Stop. Do her parents know? Is she getting a test?"

"No and yeah. Her cousin is taking her to Planned Parenthood tomorrow morning." He sighed. "Mom will kill me. How would I take care of a baby right now? Plus, she already has—"

Venni waited for more. "She already what?"

Vance fidgeted a bit. He almost mentioned Kayla. He needed a quick save. "She, um…. She already has a problem with Ava."

"Like I said before, you're a target. You have some of the best D-I schools sweating you. That's a big deal. You're a big deal. I love that you don't really see yourself that way because it keeps you humble, but you have to be smart. As grimy as it sounds, there are mothers coaching their daughters on how to trap boys with potential like yours."

"I know what you mean, but Ava's not like that."

"I don't know Ava or her mother, but I know that you might have a child on the way. Regardless of her intentions or lack thereof, that's something you don't play with."

Vance suddenly felt worse. He knew that talking about the potential pregnancy would upset his aunt. "My bad. I shouldn't have brought this up."

Venni stood and smacked him on the leg. "Stop it. We talk about pretty much everything. Right?"

"Yeah, but I know you can't have kids, and I feel bad for –"

"*What?*" Venni interrupted. "Who told you I can't have kids?"

"Mom told me a long time ago when I asked why you don't have any," he lied.

Really, he hadn't inquired about his aunt's child-free status. He loved Venni, but he was a sixteen-year-old boy who didn't care who had children unless it was a girl he was trying to get with. Tangela had voluntarily incorporated the story of Venni's infertility into her "You're gonna have a baby brother or sister!" conversation two years prior.

Venni squinted as if it would somehow help her find clarity in the absurdity of what she'd just heard. She couldn't figure out why Tangela would lie about something like that. How hard would it have been to say, "Maybe Aunt V hasn't met the right man yet"?

She had to set Vance straight as best she could for the moment. "Maybe she just didn't want to get into the conversation about where babies come from back then. But if it eases your mind a little, you haven't upset me. I am very capable of having children."

She walked to the door and stopped. "We'll figure out this thing with you and Ava. Just let me know what you find out tomorrow. Cool?"

Vance nodded.

"Alright, babe. I'm about to hit the shower. There's still some cereal down there, but if you want me to cook, I will." She smiled and winked.

"Thanks, Aunt V."

Venni closed the door behind her, leaving Vance with his thoughts. Someone was lying about Venni's fertility, and he wondered two things: Who was lying and why?

⚜

Venni took her shower, talked to Lawrence about her conversation with Vance, and waited an hour for her medicine to kick in. Once it did, she called Tangela and lit her up with a barrage of verbal shots.

"First of all, calm down and slow down. I can't understand a word you're saying," Tangela said.

"You understood what I said. Why the hell would you tell him that?" Venni asked.

Tangela laughed uncomfortably. "Girl, it was just something I came up with on the fly after he asked me why you didn't have kids he could play with when he visited you. That was years ago."

"So you told a young boy that I couldn't have children? That was the first thing that came to your mind?"

"V, you're blowing this way out of proportion," Tangela said, still laughing.

"Nah, I know what bullshit smells like, and your story reeks of it. Something ain't right. Why would you go out of your way to lie like that?"

"Oh, let's not compare lies. Keep in mind it was your lie that set everything in motion, baby sis."

"What lie? I never lied about being pregnant, and I never suggested that you raise my child. I *agreed* to you adopting Vance as your own. But if it makes you feel better to say I set things in motion, go for it. I'm setting *my lie* straight in a couple weeks. And I already set one of yours straight."

"What do you mean?"

"I told Vance I'm very capable of having children. He was walking on eggshells, trying not to hurt my feelings, when all he should've been worried about was telling me his story."

"Oh...my...God. What kind of story was he telling you that would involve your fertility?"

"Evidently the type of story he didn't want to share with you. Don't try to take this in another direction."

"What else did you tell him?" Tangela asked, nearing hysteria.

"That's it for now. I'm a woman of my word. I told you I won't tell him I'm his mother until you get here. Even though you clearly had your own shady-ass agenda, I'm looking out for my son. It wouldn't have benefitted him to learn the truth this morning—not like that."

"How honorable of you," Tangela offered, her words laced with sarcasm.

"Don't try me, Tangie. You'll fail," Venni shot back before hanging up.

⊙≫⊙

Vance wanted a hot breakfast. So, Venni found herself in the kitchen with a spread of ingredients on the newly-disinfected counter. She hoped cooking for her men would take her mind off Tangela. No such luck. Lawrence took over and kicked her out of the kitchen after she nearly diced her fingers along with the onions and peppers.

She followed his advice to go get herself together. Went into the bathroom and nursed her wounds. Took some deep breaths. Said her meditation mantra a few times. Her mind was unsettled, and so was her spirit. She couldn't shake the thought that Tangela had something up her sleeve.

After she finished in the bathroom, Venni went into every room in the house and opened the curtains and blinds. She believed sunlight emitted positive energy, and she loved to let that energy radiate through her windows and fill her house. She ended with the living room, where Vance was watching TV. When she yanked the string to open the patio door blinds, she saw blue boxer briefs on the deck, a purple bra hanging from the barbeque grill, and the remainder of her and Lawrence's clothing strewn on top of the table. Lawrence was going to be happy to hear he could change out of her basketball shorts that fit him more snugly than he preferred.

She immediately closed the blinds and thanked God for her privacy fence. She also thanked Him for the Saturday morning cartoons that Vance still loved. He wasn't paying any attention to her. Still, she needed him out of the room so she could retrieve the clothes. "Vance, do me a favor. Can you check the mailbox to see if your passport came yet?"

He hopped up and headed toward the front door. "Yep."

Once he was almost out of sight, Venni slid the patio door open and gathered her and Lawrence's belongings. She rushed back inside and made a beeline to the laundry room. Tossed the clothes onto the floor and met Vance in the foyer.

"Nope. It wasn't there," he said. "What if it doesn't get here on time?"

"Let's not even think like that, babe. I'll call your mother to make sure she sent it, though," she said.

Venni was positive now that Tangela was up to no good. She'd told Tangela about her upcoming trip to London weeks before Vance came. Though it was a business trip, she was able to take him along. She had handled all the expenses. All Tangela needed to do was make sure Vance packed his passport.

Tangela and Vance both said it was in his backpack, but when Venni told him to give it to her, it wasn't there. They'd even checked his other bags. No passport. When Venni asked Tangela to look around the house to see if it had fallen out, she said she found it and would send it. Two weeks had gone by, though. The trip was eight days away. Outside of wringing Tangela's neck, Venni didn't know what she was going to do if Vance didn't have his travel document by then.

CHAPTER 20

Great Escape

"Running away will never make you free."

– Kenny Loggins

L et's pray it's there when you get home," Dr. Cox said as she walked Venni to the door.

"Pray hard because I have a feeling it's not. And if it isn't, I may need you to corroborate my insanity plea when I choke the life out of Tangela," Venni replied.

"I will—pray hard, that is. We won't even speak the need for a plea into existence."

Venni raised her eyebrows and looked away.

"Don't let her take you there," Dr. Cox advised. "Like we discussed, you actually hold the cards right now. You just don't want to use Vance as your pawn. Sleep on it. See how you feel."

"We're supposed to leave in five days, Doc. That passport isn't in the mail. I know what I have to do."

Dr. Cox nodded. "You have my number if you need to reach me."

"Thank you," Venni said before she threw up her hand and rushed off.

Sure enough, when she got home and checked her mailbox, all she found was a stack of bills and a fitness magazine.

⚮

Tangela's cell phone rang again. This had to be the twentieth time Venni had called. She'd also called the house phone and Theodore's phone.

"What am I supposed to do?" she asked frantically. "She's not gonna stop calling."

Theodore placed two skillets in the box near his feet and reached for the packing tape. "You're supposed to pack the flatware," he answered, clearly unfazed by Venni's calls.

"I have to answer at some point."

"No, you don't. What's she gonna do, drive here and bang on the door? And be careful. She'll probably call from Vance's phone soon."

Tangela was having second thoughts about Theodore's plan to stop Venni from telling Vance their big secret. Two weeks prior, in the midst of her fury and desperation, his proposal was near-genius. Now that they were surrounded by cardboard boxes, the thrill had turned into terror. This was extreme.

"The furniture stays," Theodore said to one of the men moving about the house. "We're keeping this property."

The man gave him the thumbs-up sign and lifted the nearest box. "We'll be done in no time, then."

The movers were set to leave in a few hours. Tangela and Theodore expected to be in Great Shores, Illinois by nightfall the next day to meet them at their storage unit. Since they hadn't had much time to look for a house, they would call the extended stay lodge 'home' for a while.

Hassan said he would help in any way he could. He was ecstatic to hear that his son would be just minutes away from him instead of twelve hours. He'd already arranged for Vance to enroll in Lakeside Prep. Since he still had connections there and held a position on the school board, they didn't have to go through all the red tape to get him into the prestigious institution. The basketball coach was well aware of who Vance was and was eagerly awaiting his arrival. Theodore even had an interview scheduled there. If all went well, he would be the head of the chemistry department by the beginning of the school year. In such a short time, everything was falling into place.

Tangela honestly didn't know about Theodore's scheme at first. He didn't say a word until the second time she nearly tore the house apart, looking for Vance's passport. When he pulled it from his briefcase, she was outdone. His reasoning: Someone had to take control. Before Vance left for Houston, he took the passport from his backpack. As far as he was concerned, Vance wasn't going to London. While Venni was in London, Vance would be on his way home, ruining Venni's plans to talk to him once she returned.

The more he thought about it, though, they wouldn't be able to avoid Venni when she got back to the states. And Tangela was right. If she wanted to break the news to Vance by phone, she could. As the man of the family, he had to make the decision Tangela didn't have the strength to make. They had to move, and Vance could no longer be in touch with his aunt.

"I have to text her," Tangela said. "Something. What if she decides to tell him before she goes to London since she's pissed at me?"

Theodore rolled his eyes. "She wouldn't do that. Tell him and leave the country? Nah."

Tangela received a text. "It's her. She said, 'Since you wanna play, bring your A-game. Hope you're happy about disappointing your son.'"

"And that's exactly what we're doing," Theodore said with a chuckle, "bringing our A-game. I don't care what you say. She was setting out to hurt you. It's my job to protect you. She gave it her best shot. In a few days, she'll see it backfire."

⚜

Venni found Vance in the den after she finished packing. She was turning in early so she would be well-rested for her trip the next day. He had been quiet all evening, and she knew why. She joined him on the couch. "Well, kiddo, we tried."

"It's cool," Vance said with a shrug. He texted on his phone.

"It's not, and it's okay to say it's not. Your passport didn't grow legs and walk away. And nothing about your house is messy, so if it was misplaced or had fallen out of your bag, it would be in plain sight."

Vance agreed, but there was nothing he could do about it. "You'll be back Thursday. Right?"

"Yep. Thursday afternoon. Your mother is supposed to get here Friday."

"Yeah, she said she'd be here around six o'clock." He laughed after reading an incoming text message. "Hey. Am I allowed to have company over here while you're gone?"

"Who, Brandon and them? I don't mind. Same rules apply."

"Nah. This girl I met. Ashli."

Venni took a moment to regroup. Girl company was new. "Ashli? You've never mentioned that name before."

"I met her last week at the party I went to."

"If Lawrence is here, yes. She can come over. The days of unsupervised visits with the opposite sex are gone. You dodged one pregnancy scare already."

Vance blushed.

"And please don't sneak to her house instead. I don't need an angry father showing up here with his shotgun or finding you there. You have many years ahead, and you'll have an overabundance of opportunities to get that little thing wet." She stood and stretched. "And if Ava is still your girlfriend, you should probably break up with her before you start having female company. Don't be that guy." She winked. "Now give me my hug."

Vance stood and gave his aunt a squeeze. "Have fun," he said.

"This is a business trip, babe. You were gonna be the reason I had fun."

It was day two, and Venni had already had enough of schmoozing, shaking hands, and stroking egos. To make matters worse, she was still jetlagged and in a bit of a haze. She just wanted to close the deal on the new accounts and go home—or at least go back to her posh hotel room to get some much-needed R&R. No. She had to suck it up. She wanted to be at the top, and life at the top involved boring meetings and business politics.

She tried to ignore her buzzing phone as she sat at the conference table. She'd received six phone calls, one right after the other. When it buzzed a seventh time, she reached down and pulled it from her briefcase. After a glimpse, she could see five of the missed calls were from Lawrence. The other two were from Gabriella, who had also texted: CALL LAWRENCE ASAP then call me.

Her heart dropped. She wondered if something happened to Keyonna. Why else would Gabriella and Lawrence feverishly try to contact her at the same time? She silently prayed that Cole hadn't found her girl and done something crazy.

She and Lawrence texted.

Still in mtg.

Hate to do this to u but I need u to call me.

Be done in about an hour.

It's an emergency. No one is dead or hurt but we have a problem.

Venni tried her best to look attentive as she continued texting with her phone beneath the table.

Can call in five. Tell me something though.

Have u heard from Tangela?

No. Y?

Lawrence debated about how much he should share via text, but he knew Venni needed to know what was going on ASAP. Better yet, he needed to know how she wanted him to proceed in her absence.

I think Vance is gone.

What did 'gone' mean? Dead-gone or runaway-gone? Neither were okay. Venni excused herself and stepped into the hallway. There wasn't much privacy as the wall that separated the hallway and the lobby was glass. Venni, however, couldn't have cared less.

Lawrence wasted no time getting to the point when she called. He explained how he'd missed a text Vance sent at 10:09. He saw it shortly after eleven when he finished with his client and returned to his office. "It said, 'L, Mom and Theodore surprised me and came early. She said they'll be here in 10 minutes. Hittin' up the malls. Be back later.'"

Though he knew Vance's potential disappearance wasn't his fault, he felt guilty. Venni asked him to house-sit and supervise Vance in her absence. She trusted him with the most precious thing to her, and he'd essentially lost him. No, there was no preventing it. He was at work. That still didn't settle his spirit.

"What is that bitch up to? She wasn't supposed to be there until Friday," Venni mumbled.

"I know. That's what raised a flag for me. And I keep calling, but his phone goes straight to voicemail."

She paced in the long corridor. If it were at all possible, she would've breathed fire. "She took him." Venni knew she was right, but a part of her hoped Vance had snuck to Ashli's place against her wishes and had made up the extravagant lie about Tangela coming early to bide some time during his absence from the house.

"I just pulled up," Lawrence said, barely putting the car in park before he got out. He unlocked the door and jogged up the stairs to Vance's room. Looked in the closet. Pulled out drawers. Released a frustrated groan.

"Am I right?" Venni asked.

"Yeah. There's nothing here but his cell phone. I was hoping we were wrong." He picked it up and turned it on. "Well, now we know why his passport never made it here. Your sister had no intention of letting him go with you."

"Cowardly ass. She waited until I left the country."

"Can I even go to the cops?"

"Nope. And say what? He was kidnapped? He's legally her son. What can I say? That slimy broad had this all mapped out." Venni's volume and tone rose simultaneously, catching the attention of the receptionist on the other side of the glass partition. "And if she's as smart as she thinks she is, she'll disappear on some witness-protection-type shit, because she doesn't want me to find her or her punk-ass husband."

Lawrence read the text messages in Vance's phone. "It's obvious that Vance really was surprised. She didn't mention anything about coming early until today, right before he texted me." He searched some more. "Damn..."

"What?"

"There's a draft of a text message to you. He must've tried texting you after he texted me. It just says, 'Aunt V, Mom came,' and then it stops."

⟨⟩

"Can we go back so I can get my phone?" Vance asked.

"Vance, she's disconnecting the phones when she gets back in the States. There was no point in bringing yours along," Tangela replied.

"She wouldn't disconnect my phone without—"

"We'll get you a new phone. It's not the end of the world. Your dad and I have money just like she does," Tangela said as Theodore sped down the interstate.

"Does L know?"

"Of course he knows. From what I understand, he's moving with her."

"So he knew y'all were comin' today?"

"Yes, sweetie," Tangela lied. "They both knew. I lied to you about going shopping because I didn't want to get you all riled up over the phone. None of us wanted to upset you."

Vance sulked in the backseat of the rental car. He was totally out of the loop. Venni told him she was going to London to meet with clients, not for a job interview. According to Tangela, Venni was offered a position and salary she couldn't refuse the day before. And she accepted.

That didn't sit well with Vance. He had spoken with his aunt that evening, and they talked about everything *but* work. In fact, she insisted on not talking about business because that was the only topic of her conversations for nine hours that day. Maybe the job offer was the real reason she didn't want to talk business. Maybe she didn't want to tell him over the phone.

"If Aunt V's still coming back on Thursday, why couldn't I have just stayed until then? It's only two more days!" Vance asked.

"Exactly. It's only two more days," Tangela replied.

"At least I would've been able to tell her 'Bye,'" he mumbled.

"I hate to break it to you, son, but the world doesn't revolve around you and your aunt," Theodore said. "There's another job change occurring. You staying down here two more days isn't conducive to that change."

Vance turned the music up in his headphones and closed his eyes in an attempt to block the tears that wanted to fall. He'd heard enough and only some of it made sense. The rest was missing chunks of logic.

Minutes later, the car came to a halt. Tangela tapped him on the leg with a piece of paper. "Here," she said.

He opened his eyes and accepted the paper. Read the boarding pass. "Chicago? What's there? I thought we were going home," he said.

Tangela smiled. "We are."

CHAPTER 21

Alliances

*"If you want peace, you don't talk to your friends.
You talk to your enemies."*

– Desmond Tutu

Gabriella and Keyonna were sitting in Venni's driveway when she came home from the airport. Lawrence had filled Gabriella in on the details of Vance's disappearance while Venni was still in London, and she in turn told Keyonna. There wasn't a question about whether they were traveling to Texas to help. All they needed was their girl's arrival date and time.

The three women sat in the living room recapping Tuesday's events and Venni's interactions with Tangela during the weeks leading up Tuesday. Gabriella jotted notes on a pad in an effort to find an aha moment.

"That bitch is crazy!" Gabriella blurted.

"Certified," Keyonna cosigned.

"Vance has to be so confused. I wonder what she's telling him."

"Lies and fairytales. I'm the bad witch; I'm sure," Venni said.

Keyonna waved that off. "It's okay. Let her get story time out of her system. It's only a matter of time before you find him. She's gonna have to enroll him in school soon."

Venni let out a sardonic chuckle. "Yeah, but I'd have to contact every high school in the country. I don't even know what state they're in. They wouldn't have stayed in the D.C. area."

"Okay, so that potentially rules out Virginia and Maryland. Maybe even Philly. She wouldn't be stupid enough to go back to Chicago. Would she?" Keyonna asked.

"I wouldn't rule out any of 'em," Gabriella said. "Sometimes people hide out in the open. No one usually looks in the most obvious places. During Hide-and-Seek, I would hide near the seeker because they would never check the spots close to them. They finished counting and ran off."

Keyonna blinked a few times. "Digression, G. Come back to us."

"Y'all know what I mean. Don't even try it."

Lawrence strolled into the room without warning. "What y'all in here talkin' about?"

Since Venni was silent, Keyonna spoke up. "Just doing a little strategizing."

"Well, it sounds like y'all need to listen to G before she pulls out a straight razor," Lawrence joked. He stood behind the couch and wrapped his arms around Venni.

"Why do I have to own a straight razor, Lawrence?"

"Because you're a G! I've heard the stories. Do you keep it under your tongue?"

Everyone laughed, including Gabriella. "I'll never tell," she replied.

Lawrence's tone became more serious. "I guess y'all haven't heard anything?" he asked before he joined Venni on the couch.

Gabriella stood with her cell phone in-hand. "I need to make a phone call. Be back."

Keyonna summarized their conversation for Lawrence while Gabriella got Venni's attention. She motioned for her to meet her in the foyer before she strolled away. While she waited for Venni, she looked at one of Vance's pictures on the wall across from her. He was the one person Venni loved without reservation, and he was gone. She couldn't watch this happen to her friend again.

After a minute or so, Venni came out. "What's up?"

Gabriella peeked over Venni's shoulder before she spoke. "V, I don't think you've exhausted every option yet."

"What do you mean?"

"I'ma give you twenty-seconds to cuss me out after I say this, and that's it," Gabriella started.

Venni couldn't imagine what was coming next.

"You need to contact Hassan. Because of their agreement, he has to know where they are."

"You are outside of your fuckin' mind if you think I'm gonna get in touch with that piece of shit."

Gabriella looked at her watch and counted the seconds.

"That dirty bastard probably helped her kidnap him. Neither one of them care how I feel. I'm not his mother by their definition. I'm just the chute Vance came out of," Venni continued. "And if he *is* willing to lend his help, I'm sure he'll first want to lend his pencil d—"

"What y'all doin' out here?" Keyonna asked as she rounded the corner. She noted the intensity of their facial expressions. "What did I miss? Is there a new development?"

Gabriella held up her index finger and turned to Venni. "You had two more seconds left. You done?"

Venni clenched her teeth. Gabriella's suggestion wasn't necessarily a bad one, but Venni hadn't spoken to Hassan since her senior year at Lakeside Prep, and she was totally fine with that. Pretending he no longer existed was helpful to her psychological health. So, she was less than eager to disturb her dormant feelings.

Gabriella turned back to Keyonna. "I told her she needs to find Hassan and ask him what he knows."

"Ooooh," Keyonna responded with a grimace.

"Right," Venni agreed.

Lawrence entered the foyer. "Everything cool out here?"

Gabriella stared at Venni, who looked in the opposite direction. Keyonna shrugged.

"V," Lawrence said as he approached her.

"They think I should call Hassan," she said.

Lawrence took a deep breath. "You don't want to?"

Venni cut her eyes at him.

"Think about it, mama. Just don't think too long. Tangie's crazy ass will mess around and leave the country," Gabriella warned Venni.

"You think she'd go that far?" Keyonna asked.

"Did V ever think she'd kidnap Vance from this house and vanish in the fucking wind? They could be already out of the country for all we know."

"They aren't. I have a friend who works for the Department of State. Vance hasn't used his passport," Venni said.

"You better use those connections, girl!" Keyonna encouraged. "I agree with Gabi, though. You don't have anything to lose by asking Hassan. Call from a private number."

Venni went to punch the wall, but stopped herself. Groaned. Gabriella grabbed a fist full of Venni's shirt and pulled her closer. She pointed to Vance's picture. "Are you using my phone or yours?"

⌘

832-723-52... or was it -56... Vance tried his best to recall his aunt's phone number. She was usually Speed Dial #2. He now understood what adults meant when they said cell phones had ruined their ability to retain information.

Venni had been home from London three days, and he still hadn't heard from her. On Thursday, her day of arrival, he attributed her lack of contact to being jetlagged. Friday, he wondered if she was in-route to surprise him. Unfortunately, the only knocks on the door were from housekeeping. Now that it was Saturday, he was unsure of his feelings. It wouldn't make sense for her to not reach out, but the fact was she hadn't reached out.

Tangela said Venni was probably so busy packing that she didn't have time to breathe, let alone call them. Well, Vance had time to call her, and that's what he planned to do if he could only remember her number. *832-723-5....*

Getting in touch with his aunt had suddenly become complicated. When he asked Tangela for the number, she said

Venni had already disconnected the phones and hadn't reached out with her new number yet. When he attempted to email or Skype her, he found that the internet was blocked on his laptop. When he asked to use Theodore's laptop, it suddenly had a virus. Something wasn't right.

He stood at the desk and stared at the phone. *Were the last numbers 93 or 39? 34?* He wouldn't know until he tried. An elderly man picked up when he dialed the first number. A teenage girl picked up on his attempt at another number. He rolled his eyes while he waited for someone to pick up his next call. After two rings, he lowered the receiver from his ear. What was the point? The door opened, startling him to slam the receiver onto the base.

Tangela walked in with Kayla in her arms. "Who were you on the phone with?" she asked.

"Nobody."

She narrowed her eyes. "Don't lie to me."

Though he couldn't quite prove she'd been lying to him, he found it ironic that she was accusing him of doing the same thing.

"I was about to order pizza, but I remembered I didn't have any cash," he said.

Tangela kept a suspicious eye on him. "Go ahead and order," she said. "Get two. Theodore will be back soon."

⊙≫⊚

"What happened?" Keyonna asked as Venni moved the phone away from her ear and looked at the screen with befuddlement.

"Nothing really. As soon as I said 'Hello,' the person hung up."

"Oh. Probably the wrong number."

Venni didn't seem convinced. She stared at the number a while longer. "It's a Great Shores area code," Venni said.

"That might have been Hassan reaching out," Gabriella said.

Venni twisted her lips. "Why would he hang up? How would he get my number?"

"I don't know! Who the hell else do you know in Great Shores?"

"Cole," Keyonna said nervously.

"Please. He isn't interested in tracking anybody down but you," Gabriella replied. "Call the number, V. You've had three days to grow some *cojones* and call Hassan. Now this number has fallen into your lap. *I'm* gonna start making some calls if you don't."

Venni knew she couldn't just ignore the number. If someone was calling from Great Shores, they knew who she was. Her concern was that the police wanted to question her again about Cassidy's death. That damn case just wouldn't go away. Before she picked up her phone and called the number back, she wanted to make sure a detective wasn't going to be on the other end of the line. After performing a reverse lookup of the number on her laptop, she wasn't any closer to having answers. The search yielded no results. To help ease her mind, she searched GSPD's website for contact numbers. None of them were remotely close to the number in her call log.

Venni hesitated before she pressed *67 and dialed. A woman picked up the phone after five rings. "Hello?" she said, sounding a bit winded.

Venni didn't say a word. It was Tangela.

"Hello?" Tangela said again. She covered the mouthpiece and spoke to someone in the background. "Turn that TV down, please! I think it's the pizza man. Did you tell him the room number?"

The male voice in the background was unintelligible.

Tangela returned to the call, only to hear the dial tone. Venni had already hung up.

"Vance must've snuck and called me," she said.

"That was him?" Keyonna asked excitedly.

Venni shook her head. "Tangela. I bet she walked in when he was calling earlier."

"Maybe she's letting him visit with Hassan before they go to their final destination," Keyonna speculated.

"I'm done dealing with 'maybes,'" Venni said.

A quick search on the web confirmed that Hassan still had the same number. Venni sat on her bed, cringing each time the phone rang on the other end. Gabriella sat beside her. Keyonna fidgeted near Venni's closet and looked on.

A familiar voice sounded through the earpiece. Hassan's heavy Middle Eastern accent made her skin crawl. She didn't respond until Gabriella elbowed her. "Hassan, this is Venita." She could've sworn she heard a slight gasp. "I need to speak with you. It's urgent."

"Sure," he replied. "Hold one moment." He asked someone to excuse him while he took the call. Once he was in a different room, he expressed his surprise. "My goodness. Forgive me. You must know this is quite a shock. Are you well?"

"Listen. I need to talk to you about Vance."

"Yes. Quite the young man we have. I was happy to hear that you still respect the quality of education at Lakeside in spite of the extracurricular activities that led to some unfortunate circumstances. I know Vance will excel here, just as you did."

Venni paused. Replayed his words in her head. "Wait. What?"

Gabriella motioned for her to put the call on speakerphone. Keyonna moved in closer so she could hear clearly. Hassan went on to explain.

"Tangela told me they relocated because you insisted on Vance graduating from your alma mater. I am in full agreement with you. In my country, we also like to create legacies, and his will be one of greatness if he follows in your footsteps. He will be well taken care of here. I promise."

The three women looked at each other with disbelief. Gabriella mouthed "I told you." She figured Hassan would know where Vance was, but she never imagined he would say he was living in the same city. It made sense, though. Tangela knew Venni wanted nothing to do with Great Shores or Hassan and that under most circumstances, the city wouldn't be on her radar.

Venni couldn't believe how things were unfolding. She needed more answers, though, and she knew what she had to do to get them. Before she could tell him what was really going on, she needed to gauge his allegiance to Tangela. She softened her tone and turned on the charm before she spoke again. "Can I ask you something?" After he gave her the go-ahead, she said, "Where do your loyalties lie?"

"I don't understand your question."

"We have history. Right? Does that still mean something to you?"

"Venita, by your standards, I know you will disagree, but I have always respected you. When you became the mother of my child, I became forever indebted to you. That is the greatest blessing any human being can give to another human being. You are a part of my family."

Venni closed her eyes and took deep breaths in an effort to ignore the nausea that his words conjured up. Gagged anyway.

"Is there something you need?" Hassan asked.

Venni told him everything, starting with the dreams and ending with their present conversation. "I guess at this point, what I need from you is the opportunity to see my son and speak to him. Like I said, Tangela and Theodore have changed their numbers and the cell phone I bought Vance is here at my house. I actually need to speak with them, too."

"Most definitely. Vance was our favor to Tangela. I'm not sure why they would run off with him like that. They've created quite the plot."

Though Hassan's wording objectified their son, she understood what he meant. From the beginning, Hassan wasn't a huge fan of Tangela raising Vance.

"They ran off because they know I don't have legal rights. I couldn't say they kidnapped him," she replied.

"Yes, you could have. We are legally his parents. We have paperwork to prove it," Hassan said.

"Hassan, we're biologically his parents. His birth records don't count. The adoption papers do."

"I know."

To her surprise, Hassan revealed that he never signed away his rights. He would not complete the necessary forms for Vance's adoption to be legal. Tangela never told Venni this, allowing her to believe she was lawfully Vance's mother.

At age fourteen, Venni let the grown-ups handle the paperwork. She just wanted to make sure Vance was raised in a good home by someone she trusted, and she wanted to be in his life. At age thirty, she learned that the one person she trusted had been deceptive all along.

Venni didn't hold Hassan responsible for the misinformation. In high school, her contempt for him only allowed them to hold ten-minute catch-up sessions, during which he spent most of the time trying to pull information about Vance out of her. And those only happened because he tracked her down and called her out of her classes. This was the first real conversation they'd ever had and the only conversation they'd had during her adult years.

"I agree with you," Hassan said. "There are too many lies. He must know the truth. I have contact numbers for Theodore and Tangela. Vance does not have a phone of his own. We could—"

"You know what? I don't want their numbers," Venni said. "They'll only run again if they hear from me. Is it okay if I come to your house? Can you invite them over for dinner or something?"

"Yes. Vance will be here next Friday while my wife is at her relatives'. Tangela and Theodore are picking him up on Sunday."

"I'll be in town Saturday night. Keep it classified."

He agreed. "Do you have a specific plan?"

"I just plan on telling the truth—everybody's truth, if need be."

"It may go smoothly. Vance is old enough to decide who he wants to live with once we tell him the truth. If he chooses one of us, Tangela still has her little girl. That should—"

"What little girl?"

CHAPTER 22

Truth Hurts

*"What does the truth matter? Haven't we mothers all
given our sons a taste for lies, lies which from the cradle
upwards lull them, reassure them, send them to
sleep: lies as soft and warm as a breast!"*

– Georges Bernanos

Venni and Lawrence leaned against the wall of the garage,
impatiently waiting for Hassan's signal. He said he would
step into the kitchen and unlock the entry door when it was
time for them to give Tangela and Theodore their version of a
surprise visit. They had only been there for a half hour, but it
felt more like half a day.

Venni wiped her sweaty palms on her shorts. Readjusted
her ponytail that needed no adjustments. Checked the time
on her phone.

Lawrence held her hand. "You good?"

She nodded. "I just don't wanna hurt him."

"Mama Miles might leave her grave and come hurt you if
you don't do this," Lawrence said, bringing a smile to Venni's
face.

"Nah. We're here now. It's all coming out today."

CLICK.

Venni looked at the doorknob and then at Lawrence. He squeezed her hand and kissed her forehead. "Let's go make some waves," she said before she turned the knob.

Hassan returned to the dining room. Tangela and Theodore were still devouring the chicken and rice on their plates, while Vance picked at his food. Mashed potatoes oozed from Kayla's mouth as she kicked and giggled in her high chair. There were two other place settings that were still untouched.

"Did your friends make it?" Tangela asked once Hassan sat down.

"Yes. I believe they are fixing their plates."

Venni appeared in the archway with Lawrence at her side. "I don't have much of an appetite," she said with her eyes fixed on Tangela.

Vance's eyes widened. "Aunt V!"

Though she was just as happy to see him again, her face showed no signs of joy. "Vance, I need to talk to you."

Tangela and Theodore looked like they'd seen a ghost. Theodore set his fork on his plate and pushed his chair back from the table. Lawrence made eye contact with him, daring him to get up. He remained seated.

"Don't you move," Tangela ordered as Vance went to stand. He reluctantly obeyed. She turned her attention to Hassan. "I can't believe you."

Hassan dabbed the corners of his mouth with his napkin. "Wrongdoing has no justification. I have done my share, but

I have accepted my consequences," he turned to Venni, "and apologized for my offenses."

He had indeed apologized profusely the night before, when she and Lawrence met with him to discuss their strategy for Sunday's dinner. Before that, the last time Venni saw Hassan, he'd placed her high school diploma in her hand. The week prior to that date, he'd placed his pathetic excuse for a penis in her hand, wanting one last thrill while she was still in Fast Track and subject to Cole's orders. She was well aware of his offenses, but she'd yet to see his consequences unless his receding hairline counted.

Tangela rolled her eyes. "Suddenly you're full of integrity?"

"I was unaware of what you had done until Venita contacted me. I refuse to help facilitate your kidnapping scheme," Hassan replied.

She laughed. "Kidnapping scheme? He's my son. I'm free to take him where I please. And you're an idiot. She hates you. I've been your ally. I'm the only reason you still see him."

"No, I believe our legal documents are the reason I still see him."

"Vance…." Venni walked around to his side of the table.

Tangela stood. "Do you really wanna do this, Venni?"

Vance stood, too. "What's goin' on?" His question was directed to anyone in the room who would answer. "Y'all talkin' around me like I'm not here."

"This shit is over, Tangela. I'm done with the lies." She pointed to Kayla. "You had a baby! You had a baby and never told me."

Vance reached out and touched Venni's shoulder. "Aunt V, she just didn't wanna hurt your feelings."

She jerked her head in Vance's direction. "Your mother having a child does not affect my life. If you still believe her lie about me being infertile, you need to stop. I can have children. I already have a child."

"Don't do it, Venni," Tangela warned as she walked toward her sister.

Vance squinted with confusion. Hassan stood, but stayed near his chair. Theodore comforted Kayla, who was now crying.

Vance stood between them. "Stop! Aunt V, you had a baby?"

Venni and Tangela stared each other down. Venni looked at Vance. "Sixteen years ago." She gave him a few seconds to let her words register.

Vance's eyes asked what his mouth couldn't.

"On February 15, 1991, I had a son prematurely. I was fourteen years old."

A mixture of shock, horror, and dismay swept over Vance's face.

"Tell the rest," Tangela demanded.

Venni kept her attention on Vance. "I wasn't trying to tell you like this. There's more, but there's a time and place. If you'll hear me out."

Vance's eyes filled with water. "Why didn't—"

"She was a prostitute." Tangela spoke to Vance, but glared at Venni.

"That is enough," Hassan said.

"Go ahead and defend your ho all you want to. The facts are the facts."

"I got your ho," Venni replied.

Lawrence rushed over just in time to grasp Venni's arm before her fist connected with Tangela's jaw.

"It's time to get out of here, Tangela. Let's go," Theodore ordered as he placed Kayla in her car seat.

"Wait! Is that true?" Vance asked Venni before swiping away a tear.

"Let's go, Vance." Theodore's spoke with unwarranted authority.

Venni opened her mouth to answer Vance's question.

"Hassan isn't your uncle," Tangela interrupted. "He's your father. He liked having sex with young girls," Tangela continued.

"You are heartless," Hassan said. "I want you out of here."

She shrugged. "Fine by me. Let's go, Vance. Or do you want to stay here with the pimp and the ho?"

"I don't—" Vance began.

"Choose wisely," Tangela warned. "You can't have two mothers. You choose her, you lose me."

Vance's heartbreak was more than visible. It was palpable. Venni gripped Vance's bicep and pulled him behind her as she stormed into the closest room with a door—Hassan's office.

"Don't try to clean it up now, lil' sis! Come on back! We wanna hear the lame-ass explanation you're gonna give your *son* now. Vance!"

Lawrence stopped Tangela as she stormed after Venni and Vance. "Let them talk. You've said more than enough."

"Y'all aren't gonna make me out to be the bad guy. All I ever did was love him. All I've ever done is protect him. Now, because Venni's up to her selfish antics, she's potentially ruined him. I didn't start this, but you better believe I'll finish it. If she wants to put the truth out there, I want it all out there." She snatched her arm from Lawrence's hold. "And you look like a damn idiot. You're standing here defending a woman who had sex for sport."

"Theodore, come get your wife," Lawrence said before he walked away.

Venni's hands trembled from anger as she listened to Tangela's muffled words from behind Hassan's office door. She wanted terribly to use Tangela's neck to steady them. She knew her grand entrance would stir things up, but Tangela had taken it another level. She had taken her best shots at Venni, but Vance was the only injured party.

He paced in front of Hassan's oversized mahogany desk. His long legs only allowed for a few strides across the room before he had to switch directions. He held his fist against the opposite hand's palm, cracking his knuckles during each lap. Fought more tears.

Venni walked to the desk and sat on the edge. "Heart to heart."

Vance kept moving. Said nothing. Breathed harder. She grabbed his t-shirt by its bottom seam, stopping him mid-stride.

"Come on. The truth is out. We have to talk about it." She released his shirt and slid over.

Vance joined her, sitting a couple feet away. "Were you really a prostitute?" The pain in his eyes brought tears to hers.

She hung her head. "Not your typical one, but…yes. I had sex for money. It was a well-organized, top-secret operation disguised as a club at my high school. They called it entrepreneurship, and we believed them."

"That's not even you, though! How could you do that?"

"Honestly, V, I was chasing a thrill and enjoying my freedom. And the money was good. I got paid to do what I was already doing. I was never proud of it. It was what it was."

"This is crazy." Vance rammed his head against his fists. "And Hassan is my dad? That story about my real dad being in the plane crash and him taking on his role...."

"Lies, baby." She exhaled loudly. "Hassan was my principal. For whatever reason, he was obsessed with me. He made a deal with my boss and had access to me whenever he felt like it. He didn't believe in using condoms. My boss told me to let it slide. Tangela was the one who had been told she couldn't have kids. I felt bad for her, and I knew I couldn't effectively raise a child when I was barely into puberty. That's how she became your mother."

"Man, I don't even know who I am. I don't know who to trust. All of y'all have been lyin' to me."

"And I don't have a rebuttal. You've been lied to since the day you called Tangela 'Mama' and she answered. And our lies were intricate. We twisted every detail. When you're ready, I'll clear up everything. No question is off-limits."

Vance stood up and adjusted his basketball shorts. "Real talk, I don't wanna talk to none-a y'all." He was out of the office before Venni could say a word.

❦

Vance blew by Lawrence, who was standing near the door, guarding it from Tangela. He was devastation's mascot. The "whites" of his eyes were scarlet. Once pure; now tainted—much like his spirit. Tangela reached out to stop him, but grabbed a handful of air. She followed him.

"Theodore already put your things in the car, baby. We're outta here."

Hassan stepped in Vance's path. "Wait. I want to talk to you."

"All y'all have so much to say now," Vance replied. "I'm not tryna hear it."

Venni exited the office and joined everyone in the dining room. She stood in the entryway and leaned against the wall with her arms folded. Blinked away tears. Lawrence stood next to her, but kept a close eye on Vance. Venni's attention was on Theodore, who stood just inside the great room, eager to leave.

"Your mother and I felt it was time for you to know," Hassan continued.

"Which mother?" Vance asked.

The room fell silent. Vance looked at each of them. Excluding Lawrence, they were all strangers. The names he'd been calling them to-date were aliases. His mother was his aunt. His aunt was his mother. His uncle was his father. He was the product of a pedophile and a hooker. He stepped around Hassan and was at the front door in no time. Without breaking his stride, he pulled his baseball cap from the coat tree and left.

"I got him," Lawrence said as he rushed after Vance.

"No, you need to stay out of this," Tangela said as she followed Lawrence. "You aren't family."

"Tangela!" Theodore called. When she turned around to acknowledge him, he signaled for her to return to the dining room. Before she could protest, Lawrence was out the door. Hassan walked out after him.

Tangela started a slow clap once she was a few feet away from Venni. "Give it up for the mother of the year, everybody!

Her soul is cleansed, but everybody else has her dirt splattered on them." She clapped louder. The noise woke Kayla, who had just fallen asleep in Theodore's arms. In turn, she wailed, adding to the commotion.

"You're dead wrong for saying all that in front of Vance. You showed the hairiest part of your ass," Venni said.

"And I didn't even get paid for it," Tangela said, shaking her head. "Tell me. How many licks did it take for you to get Hassan on your team? What'd you do? Let him get a couple freebies?"

Venni charged toward Tangela until she backed her against the wall. Tangela's spine hit with a thud. She held her breath as Venni stood nose to nose with her. "It'll take one lick for me to knock your ass out, sister or not. The only blood we share is from a man who lost my respect years ago. That shit's thinner than water. Don't think I won't handle you like you're a stranger."

Theodore hurried over with screaming Kayla still in his arms. He shifted her to one side and used his free hand to grab Venni's shoulder. "Okay, that's enough," he said.

Venni snatched away. "And your self-righteous ass," she said calmly. "I know Tangela's weak ass didn't come up with this relocation plan." She stepped back and looked him over. "Do you know I know about you or are you smug enough to believe I'll never say anything?"

Theodore frowned as Venni walked away. He could barely hear what she said over Kayla's racket, but he made out most of her words by reading her lips. He thanked God Tangela couldn't see her sister's mouth from where she stood.

Tangela waited until Venni was out of striking distance before she spoke. "Lay a finger on me, and you better believe I'm pressing charges like *you're* the stranger!"

"I've got this," Theodore said, signaling for her to be quiet. He handed Kayla to Tangela and followed Venni. "Wait a minute!" he called.

Venni stood in the doorway with one foot already on the porch. Her text message alert sounded. "Hurry up. I'm going to check on my son."

He glanced over his shoulder. Tangela was seated at the dining room table, making Kayla a bottle. Though she was too far away to hear anything, he still spoke quietly. "What were you talking about in there?"

"Bianca. 1992 through 1994. You knew her as 'Star,'" Venni said.

Theodore's skin paled and his mouth opened slightly. No words came out.

Venni texted as she spoke, keeping her eyes on her phone's screen. "Mmm hmm. Two Fridays a month. Always paid with cash. Tipped extremely well. Gave her your virginity. Cried the first time she made you climax." She looked up at Theodore. "Brian Theodore Fields has secrets, too."

"Tangela can't find out," he finally said.

"She hasn't found out."

"Why didn't you ever tell her?"

"I never had a reason to," Venni replied.

"So now what?"

Venni stepped onto the porch and headed for the steps. "Now that you've attempted to keep me from my son, I'll have to reevaluate my reasons."

With no more time to devote to Tangela and Theodore's nonsense, Venni jogged to the rental car that was blocking Theodore's Jaguar. Called Lawrence to confirm his location. Peeled off.

CHAPTER 23

In Due Time

*"Maybe all one can do is hope to end
up with the right regrets."*

– *Arthur Miller*

"How are you feeling?" Lawrence asked.

Venni tucked the phone between her ear and shoulder while she finished making her hot fudge sundae. "I don't know why you keep asking me that. The last six days, you've asked and the answer has been the same. It's day seven, and my answer is the same. Like shit."

"I keep asking because one day it'll be different."

"You're so cute. I'm glad one of us thinks the glass is half full. How's he doing?"

"He's cool. You know how teenagers are. They have plenty of distractions. He played ball earlier and then came to the gym to lift. He's in the house texting somebody now."

"His appointment with Dr. Cox is next week. Right?"

"Yeah," Lawrence replied. "Wednesday."

Lawrence and Vance had a long talk after he stormed out of Hassan's house a week prior. The bewildered teen couldn't believe the web of lies his family had woven. They were the people who were supposed to love him most, but they'd hurt him beyond his conceivable threshold. They'd taught him the importance of honesty and drilled the significance of trust in his head; but in five minutes, they collectively discredited sixteen years of life lessons. As far as Vance was concerned, they were hypocrites. All of them.

He was totally against returning to the hotel to stay with Tangela and Theodore—not just because he'd learned he wasn't Tangela's biological son, but because Lawrence refuted their claims that he and Venni were moving to London. Vance knew he could never believe another word they said.

Living with Hassan wasn't even a consideration. He only visited his weird "uncle" because Tangela made him. Vance was told that his biological father died in a plane crash before he was born and Hassan wanted to maintain a relationship with him to honor his deceased brother. Even with that lie aside, there was no way he could live with that man and not disfigure his face as payback for the times he'd violated Venni's body.

And then there was Venni. Living with her would've made the most sense if her involvement didn't hurt the most. She was his go-to, his "person." He counted on her to be straight-up with him when no one else would. Yet, she was no different than the rest. She played make-believe with the best of them, building their seemingly solid relationship on a foundation constructed from scraps. Why was he good enough to be her nephew, but not her son? How could she talk to him weekly and look him in the eyes for weeks every summer and not say anything? He couldn't move in with her. It was too soon. He had too many unanswered questions.

Lawrence made him an offer on the spot: Move in with him, get some counseling, and give Venni a chance to explain herself. No pressure, no deadlines. If Vance wanted to live with him until he graduated in two years, so be it. Lawrence just wanted his little buddy to be comfortable and his lady to be forgiven.

"He still hasn't mentioned Tangela or Theodore?" Venni asked.

"Nah, not really. The envelope from Theodore came today."

"With his shot records and everything?"

"Yeah. So, he'll be officially enrolled as a high school junior on Monday," Lawrence said. "I think school starts the Tuesday after that."

"Thank you," Venni said sweetly.

"This isn't a favor, baby. It's my responsibility. It'll all work out."

⊙≫≫

"He made me come here," Vance said.

He sat wide-legged on the edge of the couch cushion with his elbows propped on his thighs. He surveyed the room. Saw Dr. Brianna Cox's name on the degrees hanging behind the desk. Ohio State and Stanford. Vance had offers to play for both schools, but he wasn't interested—just like he wasn't interested in being in the dimly lit office. This was going to be the longest hour ever. He couldn't have been there more than five minutes, but he felt like he'd been there for twenty.

"Who is 'he'?" Dr. Cox asked.

"L. Lawrence."

"Did he force you to come or did you agree to come?"

"I guess I agreed to come," Vance said. He glanced at her long enough to answer and then stared at the floor.

Dr. Cox tapped the top of his head with her index finger. Naturally, Vance looked up at her. "I have this thing about seeing people's eyes when I speak to them. Yours are gorgeous. Do you mind keeping your head up for another forty minutes?"

Vance nodded. "Sorry."

"And one more thing because I'm picky like that: 'I guess' doesn't work in this room. This is where we work on owning your feelings."

Vance exhaled audibly and shifted his position a bit. "Cool."

"Now we can chat. Tell me about Vance. What do you like to do? What annoys you? Where have you traveled? I know you're a college-bound basketball star. Do you know what you want to major in?"

Vance relaxed as they talked about all those things and more. He was surprised that Dr. Cox knew a great deal about most of the topics they discussed. Most impressive was her knowledge of college basketball. Little did he know, she had to do some research before their session so she would be able to engage with him. It worked.

"What do you want to accomplish in our sessions?"

He shrugged. "I want to know how everybody is justifying the lies they've told about who my real mom is."

"Are they justifying or are they explaining?" she asked.

"Right now, I can't tell the difference."

"Fair enough. This is still raw. Do you want to salvage your relationships?"

"Maybe a couple. My mom and my aunt. And the messed up part is you can pick either name and attach it to those titles." Though he tried his best to steady it, his voice quivered.

"If you could ask each of them one question—only one— what would it be?"

Vance took a few moments. "I'd ask Tangela why she felt like she had to kidnap me, and I'd ask Venni if she always bought me the flyest stuff because she felt guilty for giving me away."

Dr. Cox was proud of Vance for being receptive and talkative. His cooperation was the key to his healing. Because he was Venni's child *and* a teenager, she knew he wouldn't be an easy nut to crack. Unlike Venni, though, he'd opened up in the first forty minutes, trusting her when he barely trusted anyone else.

"When is Venni gonna start coming to these sessions?" Vance asked out of the blue.

"I hadn't planned on inviting her for at least another month or so. Why?"

"Just wondering."

"Have you talked to her lately?" Dr. Cox asked.

He shook his head. "Her birthday is in two days." Silence. "Do you think I should get her something?"

"I think you should do what's in your heart. Love doesn't hold grudges."

Vance picked at the skin around his fingernails.

"Listen. We have about five minutes left. Let's lay our foundation for your following visits. I conduct my sessions using your five Ws. I call them your W-5s. Who, what, when, where, and why. All about you. Some of the questions sound like they don't make sense, but dig deep for me. Do you think you can handle that?" she asked with a smile.

Vance mirrored her smile. Dr. Cox seemed pretty cool. He didn't expect her to be so relatable and easy-going. It didn't hurt that she was cute, too. "Yeah, I can handle that."

"Alright! And I got a smile! He realizes I don't bite," she joked. "Okay. Who are you? And I don't mean what is your name."

"I get what you're asking." He thought for a few seconds. "I don't know."

At first, Dr. Cox was going to ask if he needed more time to think about his answer, but when she looked into his eyes, she could tell that was his answer. She wrote it down. "What are you?"

"Hurt. Mad. Confused."

"When are you?»

"Eventually."

"Ooh…." She was intrigued by that answer.

"Where are you?"

"Stuck in the middle."

"Why are you?"

"Because an old man was obsessed with a young girl."

Her heart broke a little more with each answer Vance gave. She set her pen down and stood. Pointed to the cushion next to Vance. "May I?" As a mother, she needed to comfort him. She rested her hand on his knee. "It takes courage to be here, and I want you to know that I admire you. Your openness is refreshing and your honesty is rare. We're going to work through this, and you will be just fine."

❧

It had been seven months, and things were looking up. Vance bought Venni a beautiful card for her birthday in August, which was a sign that he hadn't given up on their relationship. In October, she attended two of his therapy sessions per Dr. Cox's request. She was able to answer his questions, even though some of the answers weren't the easiest to accept. When basketball season kicked off in November, Venni was right beside Lawrence, cheering for him and the Westlake Generals. Thanksgiving and Christmas were awesome. Venni cooked the spread for Thanksgiving, but joined her favorite guys at Lawrence's house for Christmas Eve and Christmas Day.

Many sleepovers, dinners, and outings later, March Madness was in effect at the high school level and Vance's team had just won their first playoff game. Vance stayed the night at Venni's because he had something he wanted to talk to her about the next day.

He'd been awake since seven, which was unheard of on a Saturday morning. He didn't coach himself into going downstairs to talk to Venni until almost ten. Following the smell of onions and peppers, he ended up at the kitchen doorway.

Venni stood at the stove with her back to him, sautéing vegetables for omelets. She hummed the hook to Mary J. Blige's "Just Fine" and danced to the beat. Vance's stutter steps told of his hesitation as he made his way to the center island.

As he watched Venni's private jam session, his nerves settled. He cleared his throat, startling Venni into turning around.

"Boy!" she said after flinching.

Vance laughed. "My bad. I wasn't trying to scare you."

"It's cool. You about to leave?"

"Nah…." He walked over to her and leaned against the counter near the stove. "Heart to heart."

Venni lowered the heat on the burner and took her attention away from the pan. "What's up?"

"I've been doing a lot of thinking. You know…about everything."

"Okay…."

"And I think I want to move with my mom once the school year is over."

Venni immediately felt sick to her stomach. This wasn't a conversation she'd prepared for. Even though Vance was living with Lawrence, she still saw him almost every day. He seemed to be working through his resentment, and they were just as close as they had been before the truth of his maternity came to light. Dr. Cox had even noted their progress.

Vance's declaration seemed to come out of left field, considering how he'd shown no interest in wanting to communicate with Tangela during the seven months he'd lived in Texas. Venni now wondered if he'd been downplaying his feelings for Tangela in an effort to protect hers. Worse yet, she couldn't help but think Tangela had contacted him and spoon fed him more lies that would turn him against her.

She kept her game face intact. "Okay. Well, you're old enough to know what you want and I respect your decision. I'm just gonna throw this out there. Next year is your senior year. Changing schools again won't be a good look. I'm not saying the recruiting will stop, but the big name schools are gonna wonder if that's gonna be your pattern in the future. No one wants to invest in a player who'll only stick around for a year." She turned her attention back to the food. Stirred the vegetables. "But like I said, it's ultimately your decision."

"Well, when I talked to L about it, he said I could still go to the same school since y'all live in the same district."

Venni set the spoon aside and slowly turned to look at Vance. She was greeted by his subtle smile.

"It's cool if I call you 'Mom.' Right?" he asked.

Out of nowhere, a tear dripped onto her shirt. "I don't know whether to punch you or hug you," she replied.

Vance opened his arms and grinned. Venni leaned onto her baby's chest and wrapped her arms around him. Vance held her tightly.

"I love you, boy. I always did," she said.

Vance never doubted Venni's love for him. And though the family structure he'd known for years had been destroyed, his bond with her remained unscathed. She was consistent, even when things got ugly with Tangela, always keeping his best interest in mind.

He often thought about Tangela and Kayla. He was sure Kayla was talking up a storm and running around, destroying everything in the house now. She hadn't quite hit the terrible twos, but something told Vance she was giving her parents a preview of what was to come in June. Of course, he'd never know. Tangela stayed true to her word that if he "chose" Venni, she wouldn't be in his life.

Dr. Cox helped him see that his relationship with Venni was never a choice. They loved each other instinctively and their bond was inevitable. He learned that he didn't have to apologize for his feelings, and that made him feel better about his decision. He was ready to move forward with the woman who'd birthed him and who'd influenced him in every way that mattered. He missed Tangela, but he was happy right where he was. The drama that had taken place in Great Shores caused a hell-of-a-lot of confusion, but because of it, ironically, his love for Venni finally made sense.

"Love you, too, Ma."

EPILOGUE

September 2009

Venni exited the bathroom with a cold rag on the back of her neck; her skin flushed of its color. This had been going on for a week and a half, and she was tired of throwing up. She trudged to the bed and toppled over. Lay sprawled out with her head under a pillow. Lawrence entered the room with a can of ginger ale and a paper towel full of crackers.

"Does that rag trick really work? I never knew the point of it."

"Me, neither. It's just something my mom always did." Her voice was muffled beneath the down feathers.

Lawrence laughed. "Drink this ginger ale after you recover." He sat next to her and patted her butt. "It's not flu season, baby. You know that. Right?"

Venni grumbled.

"Do you think you need to take a test?" He slipped his hands under her shirt and began to massage her back. "The pill has been known to fail some women. My mom said she—"

"It failed me." Her words were barely intelligible.

He lifted the pillow. "What did you say?"

She pointed to the bathroom.

"You need something out of the bathroom?" He leaned closer so he could hear.

"On the counter," Venni mumbled.

Lawrence walked into the room and flipped the light switch. Within seconds, he spotted the white plastic stick with the window showing two pink lines. Next to the window was an answer key of sorts. Pregnant! His face couldn't have beamed with more pride. He rushed back into the bedroom and knelt at the side of the bed.

"Those are pretty accurate. Right?" he asked.

"Mmm hmm."

"How do you feel about this? Are you happy?"

"Mmm hmm."

He stroked her hair. "Are you sure, baby?"

"I'll be happier when I stop puking."

It was safe to stretch the corners of his mouth as wide as anatomy would allow. "You can accuse me of sounding corny, but you have made me the happiest man alive." He kissed her forehead. "We're gonna have a baby."

Venni managed to smile through her discomfort. Family planning was never a thought after she had Vance. More children weren't in the cards for her. She didn't think she was the motherly type. Didn't want to be responsible for molding a life. Besides, she'd planned on being forever single, forever an auntie. But life had proven her wrong—shown her that she wasn't always in control of her own destiny. Nature had given her a second chance to get it right...from the start.

She really was okay with this. Nervous, but okay. It had been eighteen years since she pushed a person out of her body, and she'd only been an official mother for a little more than a year. But it would all fall into place. She ran her hand along the side of Lawrence's face. "We're gonna have a baby."

◈

Dr. Cox sat at her desk and responded to some emails while she waited for Venni to arrive. Venni was no longer her patient, but when she called and asked for twenty minutes of her time, Dr. Cox welcomed the chance to catch up with the woman whose harrowing tale had become an admirable success story. If it was appropriate to have favorite patients, Venni would have been one of them.

They'd kept in touch via email over the time that had passed. Dr. Cox even had the pleasure of getting to know Vance during the year they'd spent together in therapy. He was his mother's spitting image with hints of his father's features. Had the same body language as Venni during his first session. Eerie. Finding out Venni was his mother was a painful and confusing time, but he never denied one thing: He loved her, and she loved him. Dr. Cox was relieved that they were able to work through the kinks and revise their family unit.

She was also able to meet Lawrence since he was Vance's guardian at the time. She couldn't deny he was a treat to look at every Thursday. And what a man. Not only was he unfairly handsome, his spirit oozed with sincerity. Without a second thought, he'd stepped in to bridge the gap between mother and son, to be the one person who was who they said they were when Vance didn't know who to trust. And he did it for love. He did it with love.

In their last email, Venni wrote that she and Lawrence were making plans to relocate to North Carolina since Vance had committed to attending Duke University. That was a year prior. Dr. Cox wondered if Venni was coming to say goodbye.

Shortly after she gave her receptionist the go-ahead to send her back, Venni knocked on the doctor's door. Though she'd always been undeniably beautiful, she glowed with radiance as she strolled in.

"Ms. Miles!" she stood and greeted Venni with a handshake once she reached her desk. "Happiness looks good on you."

Venni smiled. "Look at you, starting already. Thank you."

"I have to admit I'm flattered that you'd want to come hang out with me."

Venni laughed. "Let's be clear, doc. I am not hanging out in this office. I'm just visiting."

Dr. Cox threw her hands in the air. "I never was a cool kid." She smiled and invited Venni to sit in one of the chairs.

"I've graduated from the couch, huh?" Venni asked as she took her seat.

"I'd say so."

"I can dig it."

The doctor shook her head, amused. "So what brings you here?"

"Gratefulness."

Dr. Cox raised her eyebrows in response.

"I know I thanked you before, but it's like…I feel free. It sounds generic, but I feel good. If you hadn't demanded the truth from me, I'd still be loving Vance under a false pretense. I'd still be married to my lies."

"Well, that's one relationship I take pride in helping to dismantle." She peeked over the desk and saw what she was looking for: Venni's engagement ring.

"He's still in the picture," Venni said.

"I was hoping to see a wedding band, too." A wink.

"In due time. Neither of us is going anywhere. The ceremony would just be a reason to dress up and dance all night."

"Have your day," the doctor encouraged. "I believe every woman needs to feel like a princess for that one day."

"But I'm his queen every day."

Dr. Cox leaned back in her chair. "Touchéé!" She looked at her with admiration. "You've come a long way, Venni. It was my pleasure to take the journey with you. I thought about you after one of my sessions the other day. Out of the blue, 'emotional arthritis' popped in my head."

"I still Google it every now and then to make sure you aren't capitalizing off my phrase."

They laughed as Dr. Cox's cell phone alarm beeped. Venni reached for her phone. "That was mine. My reminder for my daughter's dentist appointment," the doctor said.

She pulled her purse from her bottom drawer and set it on the desk. "I hate to cut this short, but…."

"I totally understand. I was just popping in." Venni stood.

The doctor stood as well. She pulled out her hair clips, releasing her curly locks from the bun atop her head. Shook the tresses into place. Pulled off her glasses. Looked like a different woman.

"Are things still going well with Vance?"

Venni nodded and smiled. "Yep. The season starts in five weeks."

"Proud mama," Dr. Cox replied.

"Right. Of a college freshman."

"Did you find a house up there yet?"

"We're hoping to close in a few days," Venni said, crossing her fingers.

Dr. Cox pouted a bit. "So this is goodbye."

"Nah. It's 'I'll email you more often.'" She swung her keys around her finger and took a few steps back from the desk. "Listen. I know you have to go, so I'm gonna head on out. I think you should ask about my W-5s again real quick, though."

Dr. Cox smiled with intrigue. They'd revisited the questions in Venni's last session, but many things change in two years. "Go for it! Who are you?" She placed her glasses case in her purse but never took her eyes off of Venni.

"An honest woman."

"What are you?"

"Relieved."

Dr. Cox hoisted the Marc Jacobs bag onto her shoulder and joined Venni on the other side of the desk. She folded her arms. "When are you?"

Venni smiled mischievously. "In seven months." She placed her hand on her belly.

"You're pregnant?" Dr. Cox's face lit up. "Congratulations!"

"Keep going," Venni said with a laugh. "Stay focused."

"Okay, okay. Where are you?"

"In my happy place."

She winked. "I like that. Why are you?"

"Because I forgave myself." Venni nodded toward the doctor. "Thank *you* for leading me on my journey."

"You drove. I was just there to keep you awake." They walked toward the door. "Now about this little one on the way...." Dr.

Cox held the door open and invited Venni to go first.

More laughter from Venni. And blushing. "Who knew?" she said. "Venni gets to do it all again."

Dr. Cox grinned with pride, and they embraced like sisters. "And she's going to do it phenomenally."

ABOUT THE AUTHOR

PORTIA A. COSBY is the author of three other novels: *Too Little, Too Late*, *Lesson Learned: It Is What It Is*, and *The Disgruntled Wives Club*. The Indianapolis native currently divides her time between the Greater Pittsburgh and Greater Atlanta areas and holds a spot on Terry McMillan's Writers Worth Reading list.

Made in the USA
Middletown, DE
30 March 2015